I, JOHN
KENNEDY
TOOLE

I, JOHN KENNEDY TOOLE

KENT CARROLL
& JODEE BLANCO

PEGASUS BOOKS
NEW YORK LONDON

I, JOHN KENNEDY TOOLE

Pegasus Books Ltd.
148 W 37th Street, 13th Floor
New York, NY 10018

First Pegasus Books cloth edition May 2020

Interior design by Maria Fernandez

Library of Congress Cataloging-in-Publication Data is available.

ISBN: 978-1-64313-193-1

10 9 8 7 6 5 4 3 2 1

Printed in the United States of America
Distributed by Simon & Schuster
www.pegasusbooks.us

AUTHORS' NOTE

This is the story of *A Confederacy of Dunces*. At first, we planned to write a biography of John Kennedy Toole, informed by the memories of the New York publisher who championed his work. However, during our research in New Orleans, speaking to those who knew him, reading the many letters sent to him from an important publisher, we discovered only slices of information about his life—especially his personal life, which he kept from his closest friends, a source of frustration for any would-be biographer. Kenny was not a famous man when he died. Documentation that might have provided the information we needed had either been lost or destroyed, and many of his acquaintances had passed away. What we did discover were the extraordinary circumstances under which the novel was finally published and became a surprise best seller and Pulitzer Prize winner. As for the rest, we used what our research did reveal, filling in these gaps as John Kennedy Toole himself might have if he were telling the story.

I, JOHN
KENNEDY
TOOLE

ONE

———

H e was humming to himself as he drove back to the hardware store. It was a perfect day, a cool, crisp sixty degrees, sun shining, a light breeze tousling the trees. He had never before felt so free. He turned on the radio and began singing along, *"Suddenly someone is there at the turnstile, the girl with the kaleidoscope eyes."* The music lifted him. *"Lucy in the sky with diamonds."* It's 1969. John and Yoko had been married six days before. His voice reached for the high notes, and he laughed to himself, wondering why he'd waited so long. He was leaving on a journey, but first, he had to conclude his business at the hardware store.

A faded old building, its entrance belied the articles inside. When he opened the door, a bell rang, signaling the clerk. The bell reminded him of Christmas, and his mother playing yuletide carols on the piano. The clerk, a nondescript older man with a mustache and tired blue eyes, asked him what he was after this time. "I've decided I do need a garden hose after all, it doesn't have to be long," he said. A few minutes later he was back in his blue Chevy Chevelle, driving faster than usual. Today wasn't a usual day. It was more like the day before graduation. He thought how fitting that bell had been.

Next stop, food. He pulled over at a roadside café and perused the menu. He wanted one of everything. That's why you should never go to the grocery store on an empty stomach. He wasn't one to overindulge—well, perhaps that wasn't true. The extra thirty pounds were a reminder of his weakness for fried food. He wasn't a glutton. He was hearty. He enjoyed a good meal and a strong drink. You can take the man out of New Orleans, but you can't take . . . Where was it that he'd heard that dumb cliché?

The waitress was sweet, not much older than his students at the university. She was comely and attentive, trying hard to please the stranger with the enigmatic smile. He sure was happy about *something*. She could tell by the way he kept humming to himself. He was different than most of the folks who came to the café, just something about him. He ate then ordered dessert. He left her a generous tip. He wanted her to remember him.

Walking back to the car, dozens of images rolled through his mind. So much to do to get ready. He'd already surprised his friends and worried his family taking off like this, leaving everyone wondering where the hell he was going. With each day that passed, he knew they must be growing more concerned, especially his mother. She'd be frightened by now for her only child. For once he simply didn't care. It's not that he was callous. This was the most important decision he'd ever make, and it had to be done right. There could be no worrying about loved ones now, or he'd ruin the whole thing. The guy who grew up being told he was "gifted," the one who excelled at everything, who could captivate a room with his wit and humor, who was his mother's joy, his friends' salvation, that guy was no longer. Someone else, someone no one had ever met before, was stepping up.

He couldn't help grinning. He remembered when he first submitted the manuscript. It was seven months after President Kennedy was assassinated. That was over now. He'd found his spirit again, and it wasn't in the pages of his novel, it was in this trip, this act of courage and selflessness that would give his life meaning. He realized there'd be some recrimination, but what great journey wasn't without peril? He'd already braved the worst of this odyssey, displaying his soul on the pages of a manuscript, only to be played with and then discarded by the literary gods, who were no less fickle than the gods of ancient Greece.

His fate had rested on the whim of a renowned editor. His offering was rejected. He was bowing down no more. It had become a game, where losers won and winners bought garden hoses from old men who'd probably never heard of *Catch-22*, and who couldn't know that standing right there in their hardware store was another kind of storyteller, one they would read about one day in all the newspapers and magazines.

He'd been on the road for over two months now. He hadn't intended to be gone so long, but he hadn't intended any of this, really. He had pushed himself to excellence his entire life and for what? A mother who wouldn't leave him alone for one goddamn minute? The woman meant well. *Yes*, he said to himself, *keep telling yourself that*, but she didn't mean well, she never meant well, she was living her life through him and he was sick of it.

His mind drifted to his hero. He envied the poor son of a bitch. His life had a proper narrative arc. That was more than he could say for his own, which felt more like Dante's Circle than an arc. There was no beginning or end, just concentric nothingness, his creative coffers empty, spent on his hero. He'd been his creator and mentor, his advocate and ally, and he wanted him to enjoy his rightful place in the world. His hero was a man of honor among phonies, a truth-teller, an instigator extraordinaire who knew his worth, understood his importance, and who would not rest until he was given his due regard. This trip was for all the heroes in the world whose courage was mistaken for buffoonery, and whose wisdom was stomped upon by counterfeit gatekeepers who wouldn't know a true leader if he hit them in the face.

Feeling vindicated, he continued driving. The gas gauge was almost on empty. He pulled into a station. While the attendant filled his tank, he went to the men's room. He was thinking about the hose again. The bathroom mirror was so filthy he could barely see his reflection. For the best, he thought. He didn't want to see the man reflected in that mirror. It might make him change his mind. He'd already imagined throwing away the hose or leaving it in someone's garden as a gift from an anonymous stranger, an act of kindness, for which good things would come. He didn't want good things, he wanted recognition, and for that, he'd have to continue the journey. When he got back to the car, he opened the trunk. The hose reminded him of summer and the sweltering heat of the French Quarter. He could smell the skunk on the beer bottles and the fat from the deep-fried oysters, he could hear the strolling minstrels and the drunken laughter of tourists lost in New Orleans's festive embrace. He felt a wave of heat despite the cool spring day, and he unbuttoned his shirt and removed his tie. The anticipation of success. He could smell it sure as he could smell those oysters. Most people would not approve, but it wasn't any of their business. This would be his moment, and no one, not his mother, not even God himself, could diminish his excitement.

Meanwhile, in New York, midtown hummed, editors were considering manuscripts. It was spring in the publishing industry, when debut authors were usually introduced to the market. Publicists awaited word from talk show producers and magazine and newspaper book-review editors. It was all about the *New York Times* best-seller list.

He had thirsted for it, too, but the midtown editor would not let him partake of its magic. He had been denied, but worse, his hero had been denied. The editor had said about his story, "It isn't really about anything and that's something no one can do anything about." He would persevere; prove that the editor was wrong. His hero would guide the opinions of important people. He would ascend to greatness, laughing as he accepted the Nobel on both their behalf. It would be a glorious day, much like today, with the sun shining brightly, refracting off the Manhattan skyline.

He imagined the press coverage, the television interviews. Men would emulate his genteel manner. Mothers would instruct their daughters to find a man like him. He would be the standard upon which others judged gentlemanly behavior. He'd be featured in the *New Yorker*, perhaps even *Vogue*. He'd have to decide whether he wanted to teach writing or English literature. He thought Cambridge across the river from Boston appropriate, but too far from New York. New Haven was better. Maybe Princeton. Both short commutes. He'd entertain in his Manhattan apartment, nurture aspiring writers. He'd travel.

He gunned his Chevelle. "Mrs. Robinson" was playing on the car radio. He sang along. He imagined his mother right now. She would be calling every friend and relative, begging them to tell her where he might be, convinced they were lying. He giggled, naughty boy. All the years of being the perfect son, the polite little gentleman who never cheated on a test, always did his homework, respected his elders, made his parents proud, was finally proud of *himself*.

He nearly missed his turnoff. The street sign was so eroded he'd have passed it for sure if he hadn't looked up at precisely the right moment. A wink from the heavens, he thought. He parked the car. It was an isolated spot surrounded by trees. He took out a pen and opened his Big Chief notebook. He started writing where he'd last left off, the words flowing across the page. Sometimes in mid-sentence he'd stop until the rush of emotion subsided. He'd never written anything this honest before. It felt good not to worry about exposition or character or dialogue. He didn't punctuate his thoughts. He didn't want to hinder them with something as mundane as grammar. This was catharsis. His hand was vibrating with the energy of the words. Guilt flickered across his consciousness, but he pushed it away.

It's 1969, the year Richard Nixon is inaugurated and on Christopher Street in New York's West Village, one Saturday evening in June, at a bar called the Stonewall Inn, a riot breaks out. It lasts all night. It is the beginning of the gay rights movement. Much farther away, Neil Armstrong is the first human being to walk on the moon. The Jets' upstart Joe Namath will upset the Colts' established master, Johnny Unitas, in the Super Bowl. In August of this year, outside the town of Woodstock, New York, there are four days of rain, sex, drugs, rock and roll, and mud. Not to be outdone, the Rolling Stones give a concert in Altamont, California. The Hells Angels volunteer security. The Stones accept. Somebody dies. A popular novel, later to be a great film about the American immigrant story, *The God-father*, is published. A different coming of age is characterized in Philip Roth's *Portnoy's Complaint*. Dwight Eisenhower and Jack Kerouac, who, as best we know, never had what surely would have been an interesting conversation, both die.

He got out of the car and popped open the trunk. He reached for the hose. He uncoiled it, admiring its smooth texture. He inserted one end into the exhaust pipe. He took the tie he'd removed earlier out of his pocket and wrapped it around the hose, securing it to the pipe, like an ace bandage. Then he snaked the other end of the hose to an open rear window, pulled it through, and rolled the window up, shutting it tightly on the hose. He walked around to the driver's side, got back in, closed the door, put the key in the ignition, took a long deep breath, and turned on the engine.

She was beside herself with the indignity of it all. It was 1976. How could they not recognize her boy's brilliance, his gifts? He'd gotten those gifts straight from her. His cultural acuity, his literary genius, his theatrical talent, he was her achievement, her protégé, who she brought into this world to edify and inspire others. How dare these insipid fools question *her*, a woman of taste and social grace, whose boy had created a masterpiece that would cause the likes of Mark Twain to bow in admiration?

She had sent her beloved's manuscript to eight publishers! Charles Scribner's Sons, New Directions, Harcourt Brace Jovanovich. The names swirled in her memory to the point she could no longer identify which was which or how many trips she'd made to the post office over the past three years, praying this time would be it. Proud of her steely constitution, she vowed to find her champion elsewhere, someplace where elegance and manners still mattered.

The unsuspecting benefactor was in his office at the college, correcting the pages of his current novel, when her majesty of the Deep South descended upon him. This was not a woman given to understatement. Hers was a world of entrances and exits, of perfectly calculated intentions accompanied by the determined drawl of a mother on a mission. He received her as a well-bred gentleman should, accepting her gift with polite trepidation.

He was growing sleepy. His eyelids felt heavy. He reached for the radio dial. His fingertips were tingling. He shook them, thinking they were asleep. The tingling seemed distant, as if it wasn't happening to his own digits, digits are numbers, fingers are digits, digits numbers fingers digits, he kept repeating his little ditty, ditty digit, he giggled. The radio, oh yes, he almost forgot, listen, concentrate professor, *concentrate*. He thought he recognized the song. Was it Bob Dylan, James Taylor? He couldn't tell. He hummed along. He began to see snippets of memory in slow motion, his childhood. He could hear his father's footsteps, tentative across the bedroom floor, as if the dear man were embarrassed by the sound of his own presence. He smelled fresh gumbo, where was that scent coming from, his tummy grumbled, or was it the car's motor? He saw Marilyn Monroe, her full mouth, he could taste her breath.

The president of the university press gripped the pen. It was 1979. His secretary had given him a letter to sign. He hesitated. If he went through with this, if he put his name on this acceptance letter, he'd be committing to something he wasn't sure he could pull off. Did he really want to publish this book? He wasn't alone. He'd been told it had been turned down by every major publishing house in New York. The manuscript had seemed to weigh more than the English dictionary, and all right, it was funny, he'd give the author that, but it was so—what was the word—*peculiar*. It would be expensive, and who the hell would buy it? He moved to sign and then stopped, still uncertain. Then he thought of that woman. Already he could tell that she'd be difficult. He imagined his staff chasing him down the hall, an interoffice lynch mob, wanting a piece of him for forcing them to endure the woman's tirades. Still, he couldn't dislodge from his memory some of the novel's great lines: "It's not your fate to be well treated, you're an overt masochist. Nice treatment will confuse and destroy you." The president of the university press told himself life is risk, not to mention he had his relationship with the book's champion to consider, a famous writer and an honored name in the South. If he went back on his word now, he'd look foolish.

Still in the car, the grande dame's son was remembering a conversation he once had with John F. Kennedy. They were speaking in hushed tones. It was a glorious meeting of minds. He leaned in and whispered something brilliant to the president. Both men giggled. He stirred slightly, coughing. School, drool, fool, he had never been a fool, his writing was always nice, did he once have lice, yes twice, no thrice, he couldn't stop rhyming. His throat was dry and sore, sore loser, he was no sore loser, he was a winner, didn't JFK just say that, or was it his mother, it was all muddled and funny, where was he, oh yes, his car, and it was hot inside, he had to open a window. He fumbled for the handle but his fingers didn't feel attached to his hand. He reached for the door, he had to open the door, or maybe he could roll down a window, or did he try that already, he couldn't get out, he felt trapped. He grabbed at the hose, yanking and pulling on it, but the fucking thing wouldn't budge. He was pushing on the windows. His body barely moved, only his eyelids fluttered as his mind imagined he freed himself.

It's 1980. As John Lennon's new song, "(Just Like) Starting Over," is climbing the charts, the legendary Beatle is shot and killed outside the Dakota, his landmark residence in New York. Norman Mailer's novel *The Executioner's Song* is awarded the Pulitzer Prize and Ted Turner launches CNN, the first all-news network and the beginning of a brave new television world.

The young downtown editor stared out the window of his office on West Houston Street, wondering how he was going to get out of this one. The woman he was talking with on the phone was offering him the paperback rights to a novel they were releasing in a few months, which she candidly admitted no one else wanted, and probably, he thought to himself, with good reason. She worked for a university press and anyone in New York's trade publishing knew that university presses didn't do fiction, let alone literature. Even as he told himself this, he admitted that New York publishing was changing, and this enterprising fellow was keen to make his mark. The literary establishment was still dominant, but there were fresh voices to be heard. *Annie Hall* and Marilyn French had moved the taste gauge. Still, he didn't hold out much hope for the galley she'd promised to send. He liked the woman and so agreed to read it as a courtesy.

The same year, the midtown editor read the *New York Times Book Review* for that week. He wasn't one to brag but inside he was grinning. As was often the case, one of his books was on the best-seller list. He prided himself on his instincts. Rarely did a book not achieve what he'd hoped for. And the book business itself was flourishing. He fed the upper middle class its literature, and lately, he was the conductor on the gravy train. He was a publishing figure of note, and he'd earned that respect.

The passenger in the blue Chevy Chevelle was dreaming of the alleyways of the French Quarter, trolling dimly lit clubs where the harlots hunted, and Dixieland jazz was king. He could feel the dampness of the night on his face and smell the cayenne and cumin hanging thick in the air. He popped open an ice-cold beer and lifted it to his lips. He was thirsty. He drank. His mind drifted to a dance hall, he didn't know where exactly, with neon colors and Elvis singing "Jailhouse Rock," and he was dancing and laughing, and he felt so free, and then his mother came storming in and took his shoes off and threw them away, and he was barefoot, then he was standing in a classroom teaching his students, and one of them was beaming, he could tell she was interested, and then his mother walked in carrying his dancing shoes, and said he could only have them if he promised never to dance again, but he wouldn't ever dance again, his breathing grew shallow, his smile deepened, is this what bliss felt like, he wasn't sure, he was floating now.

The young downtown editor worked for one of the most influential, independent publishing houses in New York. The owner had risked his fortune by defending novels such as *Tropic of Cancer* and by winning a set of legal battles in the Supreme Court, fights that effectively ended censorship in America. The owner was listening to the young editor explain why he wanted to acquire the novel.

The man in the car was letting go. His heartbeat had slowed, his blood pressure was dropping. He was flying, the colors were swirling around him like Popsicles in summer, melting, melding, he could see everything now, the glimmering surface of Lake Pontchartrain, the discarded beads of a Mardi Gras celebration peeking through a dirty puddle, his mother's powdery skin, his father's old slippers, he felt no pain, the colors were moving through him now, coming out his fingertips.

The downtown editor was dismayed and angry. He had put his reputation on the line for this book and the university press releasing it in hardcover wasn't doing anything to promote it. The sales director had dropped this news on him, a week *after* he bought the rights. What on earth were these people thinking? Who releases a title with no mention in the catalog? There was no publicity planned, no marketing or promotion, nothing, and the initial print run was a meager two thousand copies. Why had they chosen to publish it in the first place? It was akin to having a baby and leaving it on a doorstep.

The driver was slumped over the steering wheel. His arms lay motionless at his sides. His cheeks were rosy and he was smiling. He was imagining that he was talking to his mama. He was telling her he was sorry they'd quarreled and he hoped she'd understand his reasons for this trip. He'd left the note, more of a letter really, and he didn't think she'd mind about the grammar. As the carbon monoxide filled his lungs, he thought, perhaps just this once, she wouldn't judge him.

It was now the spring of 1980. The president of the university press reluctantly authorized another print run. How many was it so far, five, six? They'd already sold almost twenty thousand books. He'd been dubious when the downtown editor had told him his plans. He believed in practicality, but the perilous terrain of risk and reward was for New York publishers, not Southern universities with a board of trustees to answer to. The downtown editor had been persuasive if not downright pushy, but he had to admit, he'd done extremely well. His division had never before gotten this kind of critical attention from major newspapers and magazines. They were the talk of university presses everywhere.

The call came into the police station just after lunch. A possibly abandoned Chevy Chevelle was parked in the woods. The sheriff wanted to send someone else to check on the vehicle, but there wasn't another officer available. He called his daughter to let her know he'd be late picking her up at school. She was a freshman at the university and he'd promised to drive down and take her to dinner that night. She was excited about her classes and he was eager to listen. He planned to leave early, avoid traffic, but not now. When he arrived at the scene, the blue Chevy Chevelle was still, the engine dead. He approached the vehicle and touched the hood. Cold. Inside, collapsed in the driver's seat, he saw the poor guy. He was a handsome lad, cherubic, ample, and the expression on his face one of content-edness. The interior of the car was pungent, but he'd smelled much worse in his time. Next to the lifeless passenger was a copy of *The Collected Works of Flannery O'Connor*. His mind drifted back to his daughter. She had recently told him she was reading that author for her literature class. Also in the car, next to the body, was a Big Chief notebook, the kind he himself had when he was a kid.

He returned to the squad car and radioed the coroner. The poor bastard couldn't have been much more than thirty years old. He was so well dressed, too, starched white shirt, pressed pants, polished shoes. He remembered the phrase "all dressed up with nowhere to go," wondering how anything could be so bad it would make someone do such a thing. He pondered the young man's family. Did he have a girl waiting for him somewhere, a mother or father? He couldn't touch the body of a corpse until the coroner arrived, but it wouldn't be against pro-cedure to search for a wallet. He reached inside the deceased's jacket pocket, nothing. Then his pants pocket. He felt the wallet. The name on the driver's license was familiar. He'd heard of this guy. He searched his memory, trying to determine where he'd seen the name. His daughter. He remembered her telling him about her literature professor. Tonight, he'd have to tell his daughter that the professor who inspired her had taken his own life. Perhaps he'd leave that part out, only tell her he'd passed. No, he thought, I'll have to tell her the truth.

The coroner arrived at the scene. A nondescript older fellow with bushy eyebrows and stooped shoulders, he opened the driver's side door and examined the body in the car. No need to feel for a pulse, he thought. Rigor had already set in. He started filling out the mandatory forms.

The small handful of people at the funeral home didn't speak much. The mother was too distraught to attempt conversation and the father stared into the distance, repeating it was cold outside for this time of year, and how his son would need a sweater. In the eyes of the church, the deceased had disgraced himself. Mourning was for the deserving. The parish priest was hoping this pitiful little display would end soon so he could return to serving the righteous members of his flock.

The service was quick and efficient. There were no wailing spectators, no flashing cameras, no reporters hastily scribbling notes, no music, no fanfare, just three people standing in a cemetery, as stiff as the body lying in the casket before them. The mother kept turning a small scrap of paper over and over in her hand. It was torn from a copy of the coroner's report. She kept reading the same line over and over. Name of Deceased: John Kennedy Toole.

TWO

⁓◦⁓

He could hear the squeaking of chairs, as the glassy-eyed recruits tried to concentrate but couldn't, their attention drifting to the balmy temperature outside the barracks, the beach, and better days. He tried to engage them, infusing humor into his recitation of past imperfect, continuous past, simple past. His students seemed distracted. Or perhaps he was the distracted one, as his novel gestated within him. He could feel it kicking.

"I am, you are, they are . . . ," he continued. One of his students smiled meekly, his body language begging the instructor not to call on him. No more than twenty years old, he reminded the instructor of his father when he was young and handsome, before he turned into the stranger who flitted about his home. Corporal John Kennedy Toole felt pity for the student, who, like most of the young men stationed at Fort Buchanan in Puerto Rico, had volunteered for military service so they could feed their families. Most were from the mountains and work was scarce. These boys weren't patriots. They were kids sitting in a sweltering room, trying to learn enough English to survive the battlefield. They were hoping it wouldn't come to that, just as their instructor was hoping he could get this damn novel out of his head and onto paper. So, there they were, a couple dozen boys who hadn't yet known the horrors of war, because if they had, they'd sure as the sun would set not be sitting in those desks, and the instructor knew this, knew that if he didn't put his whole heart into teaching these kids English, they could die one day, and it would be his fault. These were his recruits. They were counting on him even if they didn't know it.

"I am!" he said, loudly this time. "You are!" Then he told them to repeat it. "Again," he said. "Again!" The recruits seemed surprised by the sudden burst of intensity but did as they were told, while the instructor willed himself to stay on task, as characters he hadn't fully formed danced and fretted to be loosed onto a blank page.

It is November 1961. John F. Kennedy has been president for nearly a year. The Soviet Union has just conducted the largest nuclear test in history and Americans are building bomb shelters while the beatniks preach peace and love. The Orient Express makes its last journey from Paris to Bucharest as a generation of babies discover the first disposable diaper. Construction has begun on the Berlin Wall while the

Professional Golfers' Association tears down another when it eliminates the whites-only rule. It is a world struggling to adapt, caught between old-school values and the demands of an aggressive new era.

Corporal John Kennedy Toole surveyed his classroom. Tall and handsome, with a strong handshake and refined Southern manners, he was a gentleman's gentleman, an anomaly in this place. Always perfectly groomed, smelling of clean, fresh soap and Brylcreem, Corporal Toole always strived to set a good example for his students. He felt a kinship with them. Admittedly, they were uncultured. His mother would have been appalled by their lack of manners, their disregard for all things of beauty and grace. His mind was drifting again. "Focus," he thought. "Focus on these young men." All he could hear was his mother's voice, invading, always invading his thoughts like the damn mosquitos here, the size of birds. Ignatius would have stormed about the barracks complaining.

Corporal Toole suddenly began to experience gastrointestinal distress. Or wait, was that Corporal Toole or Ignatius? It was getting to the point he couldn't tell the two apart. Sometimes he found himself in a situation in which he'd normally be cool and calm, an ordinary circumstance by any civilized person's definition, and then Ignatius would pop out like a rotund, black-haired jack-in-the-box, spewing opinions. When he'd become excited, his large round eyes would bulge, animating his face.

Ignatius was more than a fictional character to his creator. He was the person John Kennedy Toole wanted to be.

"Sir, you alright?" asked the same young man who reminded him of his father.

"Yes, I'm afraid I got a little distracted," the instructor said. "I'm working on something in my free time and it does vex me."

The boy looked at his superior and smiled knowingly, even though he wasn't certain what *vex* meant. A good Catholic boy whose mother had raised him to be polite, he didn't want to disappoint her here in an army barracks where all he could think about was how much he missed everyone back home.

"Sir, what is *vex*?" asked another recruit sitting toward the back. This boy was different from the rest. He had a curiosity his superior officer admired, a desire to be something more than a poor kid who was only in the army because there weren't any other options. The instructor explained *vex* to him. The recruit nodded, listening intently. The corporal wanted to take his class in another direction that particular morning, teach his students something of substance, not just have them conjugate verbs so they could learn military commands that washed the humanity clean out of them. This corporal didn't believe in war, didn't believe in upheavals or bloodshed. If he wanted war, he could go back to Audubon Street in New Orleans and listen to his mama. That was Ignatius, *he* was the one who thirsted for revolution, who conspired to impose geometric symmetry and moral decency upon the masses. Ignatius was itching to teach the corporal's class that morning, but the corporal held his ground. This was his class and he wanted to introduce his students to the things his mama had taught him to appreciate: the theater, great literature, music.

The shy recruit inquired what he was working on that vexed him. The corporal couldn't help but smile at the lad's earnestness as he tried to form his question alternating between broken English and Spanish. Corporal Toole patiently helped him with each word, pausing to let the boy practice his pronunciation. After all, he thought, elocution is the hallmark of a refined fellow, and this instructor-cum-army-corporal was determined his recruits would leave this cultural desert more enlightened than they arrived.

"I was vexed, he was vexed, you were vexed," the student continued.

"Excellent!" Corporal Toole said. "Please continue."

Though he fought to stay in the moment, Corporal Toole was no match for the pontificating fatty in a hunting cap and scarf surreptitiously vying for his attention. He chuckled to himself remembering a recent evening. He was enjoying a perfectly convivial conversation with some of his colleagues at the officers' club. They were discussing Henry Miller, whom the corporal considered one hell of a writer, someone who could infuse a coward with an adventurer's daring. Miller validated the erotic wanderlust the corporal hungered to explore but couldn't in an army barracks, shackled by duty and honor and fear that if he did give in he would be devoured. He remembered masturbating the night before. He pondered whether Ignatius should masturbate or if the image would be too much for the reader. He longed for a female.

"Kenny, what are you doing!" his mother shouted, opening the door to his room. A shrewd, ample woman, when she spoke, she trilled her *r*'s like a second-rate Katharine Hepburn. He hastily zipped up his pants, wondering if she could see the beads of sweat dotting his forehead or the sticky substance on his palms.

"I heard you moaning and I thought you had that vexing sore throat again," she said. "Shall I make you some tea with honey?"

"What vexes you, sir?" the young recruit repeated, enunciating each syllable.

The corporal cleared his throat in an attempt to clear his thoughts. "I wrote a novel," he said. "Actually a novella." They leaned forward, wanting to hear more. Ignatius puffed with pride. His creator was about to unleash his brilliance for these students to experience.

"Yes," he continued. "It's about a young boy who does a horrible thing for what he believes with his whole heart is the right reason."

"Wait a minute," Ignatius growled. "You're supposed to be talking about me! These impressionable souls require *my* genius and inspiration!" Ignatius complained at his creator, flailing his flannel-covered arms, desperate to be acknowledged.

The corporal ignored him, knowing he'd pay later when he needed his creation to come alive on paper again. He told himself that soon he would expose the world to Ignatius. Just not yet.

The corporal chided himself for not being able to light on a single thought for more than a blink. His memory once again returned to that evening at the officers' club. He heard himself speaking to his fellow instructors and was surprised with what came out his mouth. "Henry Miller is the death of Fortuna herself and a scourge upon us all!" He then emitted a robust belch. A fleck of discomfort appeared on some of his colleagues' faces before they all burst out laughing, thinking John was mimicking someone from down South again. They awaited his next bit, grateful for the laughter he provided in a place that felt strangely like purgatory.

As the weeks turned into months and Pat Boone chased Rick Nelson on the Hit Parade, *The Beverly Hillbillies* made fun of America's growing nouveau riche, and the first Walmart opened its doors, John Kennedy Toole yearned for the comforts of home. Despite his mother driving him batshit crazy, he had to admit he did miss her cooking and the way in which she encouraged him when he felt directionless. He also missed the tiny puffs of talcum powder, delicate little punctuation marks that announced her arrival and departure from a room. Some women left lipstick prints on their coffee cups. Thelma marked her territory with rose-scented talc.

The monotony at Fort Buchanan was both a blessing and a curse. Since he'd been promoted to sergeant and given private sleeping quarters, he had a place to work on Ignatius and the cast of characters who would fuel his hero's misadventures. Sergeant Toole could lose himself in his writing, subjugate his homesickness into the more profound calling of authoring a work that would define his legacy, get him out of dire financial straits, and provide the accolades of which he was deserving. He sounded like his mother again.

The sergeant grew up worried about money. Mother preferred appearances over the benefits of a sound, realistic budget and his father was fading, his drive and desires crushed, with little remaining of what was once a good and decent man. The sergeant often wondered about his father's inner life, if beneath the innocuous chatter there was a strong human being in remission who still had dreams. The sergeant's mother reminded her son in letter after letter that his parents were near destitute and beseeched him to rescue them from the specter of poverty. Just once he'd like a day to go by that he didn't have to worry about them and then feel guilty for being angry. It was debilitating. He wished he could shut the noise off in his head but there was so much of it between his mother, Ignatius, his students' attempts at English. He could feel a dark mood rising within him. It had been worsening since Marilyn's suicide. He remembered how sweetly she sang "Happy Birthday" to President Kennedy and how he wished it had been him she was serenading. She was the angel to whom he whispered his deepest secrets from afar, hoping his affection might somehow breeze through her window on one of those claustrophobic Puerto Rican nights. How could she do that to him, be so selfish as to take her own life and deprive the world, okay, he didn't care about the world right now, how could she deprive him of her beauty, her grace, the vulnerability that awakened the hero inside of him.

He was spiraling again. He wasn't losing his mind. He was there, just burdened by forces beyond his control and so he did what he always did to wrest that control back. He took out a fresh sheet of paper from the sheaf on the windowsill. He carefully inserted the paper into his buddy's typewriter, which thank God he was letting him borrow. He hadn't told anyone about his clandestine evenings spent with the typewriter, not even his parents. The words flowing out of him were private, he wanted it just for himself, just for a while. He pushed the lever on the typewriter to the left, delighting in the clicking of the carriage. Then he escaped into the New Orleans he didn't tell his mama about, the one that breathed life into characters that were alien anywhere else in the world. As memories of his city danced in his head, he transformed them into whole living people existing in a universe of his making, where mothers were imperfect, cops wore yellow tights as punishment for picking up grampaws, and the ghost of Boethius grinned as an unlikely champion spewed soliloquies, imposing himself on the unprepared who were better for it but just didn't know it yet. The sergeant's fingers flew across the typewriter keys and if anyone had walked past his room and his window had been open, they would have heard John Kennedy Toole whistling to himself.

Occasionally, he would take a break and indulge his predilection for literature. He favored Flannery O'Connor. He was reading "A Good Man Is Hard to Find." As the children are being murdered while the grandmother rambles on about Jesus, he could feel his loins warm inside his clean cotton underwear, army issue. How he loved that woman. Flannery O'Connor. He played with her name on his tongue. She didn't give a damn about literary convention. She took the short story somewhere that was equal parts menacing and fabulous. John also felt a connection to her because they were both raised Catholic. John, how he referred to himself when he felt more like the man than the boy, fantasized about the conversation that he and Flannery might have one day about faith.

Great artists were created not born, and New Orleans created John Kennedy Toole just as Flannery O'Connor was created by her strict Catholic upbringing, her frail health engulfed by religious zealotry, and the purity of her genius that made the sergeant's cock hard and his resolve deepen. He got up and washed his hands. On the dresser was another letter from home. Reluctantly, he tore open the envelope.

He was only twenty-five years old yet felt decades older than his years. Perhaps it was the product of having students to whom he was obligated to play the role of authority figure. It didn't leave much room for the fancies of youth. He was the parent at home, too, taking care of Mom and Dad. He'd had to declare them as dependents and ask the army to distribute his wages and give them a subsidy. By the time it had all been finalized he was on edge. His moods, the peaks and valleys, were not a matter he discussed. He was creative, after all, and weren't such people prone to intensity? I'm sure, he said to himself, that Evelyn Waugh wasn't always jovial. "The womb is the darkest place on earth, and yet look at the tiny miracle that emerges from it," he told himself. "Of course, I'm going to have dark moods. It is both the privilege and the burden of every great writer. We are nothing if not for the toils of our enlightenment," the sergeant whispered to his adopted

brethren. Then he remembered a saying he'd heard somewhere, though he couldn't be certain where. "It's always darkest
before the dawn." Dawn, what a lovely name.

Yes, the letter. He began to read. His mother's words went
straight through him. His father had shingles. He could feel
his own skin itch. He had read about this insidious reiteration
of chicken pox. For a moment, he tried to remember if he'd
ever had chicken pox. He shuddered. He wished he could
do more for his father. He loved the man, though he could
never understand how someone who'd known the realities
of war, built a respectable name for himself, and genuinely
cared about others could become a footnote in his own life.
He had always been a burden and a disappointment. It made
Kenny sad.

By late November 1962, Sergeant John Kennedy Toole was
desperate to go home for a visit. He needed money for airfare
and for the first time in as long as he could remember, he asked
his parents for help. His mother immediately sent him what
she could, and between her contribution plus what he was able
to squeak out of his paycheck, he purchased the tickets. The
morning of the flight he had doubts. The sergeant's parents
were a challenge and watching his father deteriorate ate at him.
He thought of his mother's pink rouge and how it made her
appear permanently flushed with excitement. He considered
the elaborate hats she always wore that looked as if they might
take flight if startled, and he laughed, piquing the curiosity
of other passengers as they made their way to their seats. He
smiled as he fastened his seat belt. He was eager to tell her

about the novel he was laboring over. He had given one of his fellow instructors at the base an excerpt to read. The man had praised the writing and allowed how engrossed he'd been in the characters.

The sergeant's first attempt at a novel hadn't garnered such accolades. In fact, his mother never even knew about *The Neon Bible*. He'd written it for a literary contest when he was fifteen years old. He practiced the characters' dialogue aloud in his room at night, hoping nobody would hear him. Aunt Mae and the preacher were the hardest to do quietly. Kenny thought surely he'd win the contest or at least receive an honorable mention. All he got was a form letter thanking him for his submission.

Perhaps when he got home, he thought to himself, he'd reread it.

<hr />

The barracks were nearly empty. The majority of recruits had gone home for Christmas. Most of the instructors had also vacated the base, some venturing to nearby islands, others returning home to their families. Sitting in the mess hall engrossed in conversation were one of the sergeant's students and the instructor to whom he'd given the first chapter of his manuscript. The student was telling the instructor how the sergeant had been distracted for weeks, that he lost some ring he got in college, and kept asking everyone if they'd seen it.

"Did he say what college the ring was from?" the instructor asked.

"I think it was Tulane," the student replied.

The instructor understood immediately why that would bother John. He prided himself on having graduated from the so-called Harvard of the Deep South. Losing that ring must have felt like losing a part of himself.

"Since we're on the subject of Sergeant Toole, has he told you that he's working on a novel?" the instructor asked.

The student told him yes, that he'd mentioned he wrote a story about a boy who had to make a hard, awful decision. The instructor realized they couldn't have been talking about the same book. He felt a tinge of guilt for saying anything, but he was curious if John had shared the manuscript with anyone other than himself. He'd never admit this to John, but he was not impressed with the excerpt. Of course, he told John that it was wonderful, of course he extolled its virtues. He didn't want another instructor being discharged due to mental distress. It was bad enough they had an alcoholic teetering on the edge of despair. Good lord, though, he couldn't imagine how this thing the sergeant was writing could have any commercial appeal. The protagonist was a fat, offensive bore and the story seemed incomprehensible. Far be it from him to discourage the author. He would have to learn on his own that there are only so many Cervantes out there, and he, Sergeant John Kennedy Toole, was certainly not one of them.

Back from his visit home, Sergeant Toole was now one of the men in charge of the company and responsible for enforcing discipline. It was disheartening, as these young recruits needed encouragement more than punishment. When he was asked to take on English classes again because they were short on instructors, he was grateful for a reprieve.

The winter months passed quickly. Each day his writing became more personal. He was physically present, but all he could hear were the sounds of his novel coming alive. He was struggling with two of the female characters at the moment: Irene Reilly, Ignatius's mother; and Myrna Minkoff, his nemesis, who would save Ignatius from a horrible fate in the end that Irene attempts to orchestrate. He was still working through how to make that aspect of the plot work, as he wanted Irene to remain a sympathetic character despite this twist. Mothers were always complicated, he thought. John was also concerned that parts of the story didn't seem connected to the whole, but he was becoming attached to all the characters and hesitated to discard any, as it would feel as if he were putting up his children for adoption after he'd started raising them. So he tried to figure out how to give each character a purpose that led somewhere as he wrestled with the same question of his future.

Sergeant Toole still made time to socialize with his colleagues at the officers' club and received numerous commendations for his exemplary performance of duties. He was rewarded trips to Aruba and later the Virgin Islands that afforded him a welcome break from the monotony of the barracks. To everyone around him he seemed to be thriving, but inside he was restless as the novel tugged at him, begging for his attention. As he became immersed in the characters, the humor in his letters home took on a cruel patina. He no longer seemed to delight in observing others unless he was mocking them. A gifted mimic, he'd often made fun of people. Even his friends weren't immune.

Tensions mounted as morale at Fort Buchanan withered. Perhaps it was the increase in inspections or the rumors that the base might be closed that were interrupting the drumbeat of ritual in the barracks. Or maybe it was Sergeant Toole himself who was ready to flee and resume his life back in New Orleans. He'd already written friends requesting that they find out if there were any available teaching posts at the better private schools. Though he considered going back to New York to finish his graduate work at Columbia, he realized that his novel needed the sultry embrace of his cherished city. He also knew that living in New York again would drain him financially and leave little time for writing. His decision made, he purchased a fine typewriter of his own, an Olivetti.

As the torrential Puerto Rican rains subsided and winter surrendered to spring, John was no longer Sergeant Toole. He was John Kennedy Toole, an author living vicariously through his character Ignatius. Then one night the curtain fell.

One of the instructors in Company A attempted suicide. Sergeant Toole had never taken a liking to the fellow. No one had. His speech and mannerisms suggested that he might be gay and inspired ridicule and contempt. As he lay on the floor of the canteen, his skin clammy and pale, Sergeant Toole did nothing. His comrades anxiously awaited their leader to summon an ambulance or a doctor, but the man they'd come to admire and revere, who'd protected them from overzealous superiors, engaged and entertained them on days that threatened hopelessness, the one person who made life bearable in this often unbearable place, just stood there.

The silence was palpable. Sergeant John Kennedy Toole finally walked to the phone and made the lifesaving call. Someone murmured a prayer from the back of the room. That night he couldn't sleep. He kept reliving what had happened and wondered why he had waited. He remembered feeling frozen, like a small child watching another child drown, afraid to summon the adults for fear they'd both get into trouble. Eventually, he would tell himself that his hesitation to get help was an optimistic reflex, that he was convinced the man would come to on his own and he wanted to spare him any embarrassment. That's what he would tell himself but he would never be certain.

Three months later, in August 1963, as Beatlemania continued to entrance the country, President Kennedy and the First Lady mourned the death of an infant son, American would-be defector to the Soviet Union Lee Harvey Oswald was arrested and released from jail, and the Reverend Martin Luther King Jr. captivated a generation with his "I Have a Dream" speech, Sergeant John Toole boarded his flight home, his military duty completed. He fell asleep the minute of takeoff, his memories of Fort Buchanan escaping into the ether. He awakened to the stewardess's voice over the loudspeaker, informing passengers the plane was in its final descent and to prepare for landing.

THREE

⸺✦⸺

Flashback to a balmy autumn morning in
New Orleans, an apartment on Webster Street.

High school freshman Kenny Toole, twelve years old, was getting dressed for school. He was practicing his morning smile in the mirror, making sure it was convincing enough that his parents wouldn't worry he might be sad, which he was. Kenny didn't want to disappoint his parents, especially his mother. She had sacrificed friendship, evenings out with her husband, and beautiful dresses so that he could skip two grades, and she had continued sacrificing to ensure her child would stay ahead of his peers. She had hoped to hire a tutor and was taking on extra work, but it wasn't enough, so she tutored Kenny herself.

There were nights she'd stay up long after her husband and son were asleep, reading and prepping his lessons. Kenny knew how much his mother loved him but sometimes he just wanted to be a regular kid.

Thelma repeatedly told Kenny that he was a prodigy whose superior talents were to be nurtured and developed and not squandered on stickball. He was led into art, theater, music, the finer things. It wasn't that Kenny didn't enjoy those things, but he wanted to know what it might be like to play outside and come home muddy with grass stains on his clothes or to build a tree house with some of the neighborhood boys, where they would hide girlie magazines and stare at the pictures, giggling. Yes, he liked the stage, and when mother wanted him to perform in her plays and pageants, he went along and even enjoyed the attention. Sometimes, though, he felt his mother couldn't seem to love the boy secretly struggling to live up to her ideal of the perfect son. His dad wasn't like that. His dad taught him about baseball players and cars. Once, when Kenny was six years old, he let him drive the family Oldsmobile around the block. Thelma was so angry her hands shook.

These days, Dad was physically present but his mind wasn't right. Kenny couldn't always understand where his dad was even when he was standing there in front of him. He was retreating into his own world a little bit more every day. Kenny's mother tried to protect her son from the truth of her husband's illness, but twelve-year-old boys are clever in ways that grown-ups seldom realize. He knew there was something amiss. His classmates' moms didn't work. They were homemakers. The fathers were the heads of the household and supported the family. His mother worked hard. Kenny heard her crying at night sometimes. He wanted to comfort her but was scared she would tell him things he didn't want to hear, like his dad was getting worse and that she was afraid. As Kenny buttoned his crisp, clean white shirt, he noticed his dad lingering in the hallway talking to himself about the lock on the front door, that it needed to be replaced. That lock was brand new.

The year is 1950. The average cost of a new car is fifteen hundred dollars and a gallon of gas is eighteen cents. Eight million homes in America now have television sets. A fresh actor in a Pepsi commercial named James Dean will begin to fulfill his destiny five years later in the film *Rebel Without a Cause*. Diners Club issues the country's first credit card and McCarthyism casts a pall over an otherwise optimistic nation still recovering from a world war.

John Dewey Toole wore what was left of his potential with dignity. His once powerful frame, now shrunken, as if in apology, belied the integrity of his character. He loved his boy and wished his wife wouldn't be so hard on him. He wanted to protect Kenny from the ills of living in that house where he'd already become a ghost. What kind of father, he would ask himself, prays their child will run away? Some days J. D. Toole felt human, as if he'd reentered his own familiar mind. In those dwindling moments of clarity, he'd shudder, realizing he was dressed in only his undershorts and slippers but by the time he'd get to his closet for his pants, he'd be too distracted by the locks to remember why he was rummaging through his clothes. He'd try to tell his wife what was happening to him, but Thelma wasn't an easy woman to talk to. She'd pat his hand and change the subject to happier times. Perhaps it was the way in which she spoke to him, but every so often he'd almost seem himself again and she'd whisper something only meant for a husband and he'd smile. Other times, he'd snap at her, which they both knew was unlike him.

Kenny opened his bedroom door and looked at his father, searching for a glimmer of the man who had shown him how to pitch a fastball.

"Remember, son, grip the ball gently. That's right, good, good. Now, pull back, concentrate, and throw!" Kenny was trying so hard he tripped, sullying his trousers. He looked away as he fought back tears.

"Son, you did fine! Come here, let me help you with your stance."

Kenny was lost in the memory while J. D. Toole began fidgeting with the window in his son's room, making sure it was locked, becoming agitated.

"It's okay, Dad," Kenny said. "Let's go see if Mom has breakfast ready."

John Dewey Toole dutifully followed his son, the pads of his slippers flapping on the hardwood floor as he contemplated every window and door and whether they would protect his family from a marauding intruder. Though John Dewey Toole still went to work a few days a week, Kenny couldn't help but wonder how he was getting anything done. He'd heard his parents arguing about money, and his mom pleading with his dad to see a doctor. Kenny had never told anyone, but lately his dad had started coming into his room in the middle of the night confused, asking Kenny if he'd like to hear a bedtime story. When Kenny was three years old, *The Tale of Peter Rabbit* was his favorite book, and every evening before bed he would beg J.D. to read it to him. His dad would lovingly tuck him in, and in a soft, melodic voice soothe Kenny to sleep with images of mischievous Peter Rabbit and mean ole Farmer McGregor. Then, J.D. would quietly slip out of his little boy's room and retreat to the kitchen, where he'd make himself a cup of hot tea and review his to-do list for the next day. He wanted to be the type of man his wife could admire.

"Are you certain you want this make and model?" John Dewey Toole asked his customer. The man had been at the dealership for nearly two hours, hoping to purchase the perfect set of wheels. J. D. Toole had one of the best reputations in the car business. His clientele trusted him and relied on his judgment. Most times, he'd recommend a vehicle and the customer would go along with whatever J.D. suggested. This fellow was different. He worked in the utilities business and had recently been transferred from Chicago to New Orleans. Though he spoke animatedly about his new job and the opportunity it afforded him, J.D. thought something awry. J.D. grew up on Sherlock Holmes mysteries and was fascinated by the detective's ability to extrapolate whole stories from the tiniest detail. His customer had large circles under his eyes. He was dressed in a bespoke suit that now hung awkwardly on his gaunt frame. The elbows were worn and the tip of the lapels had started to fade.

"Please, let me show you one more option before you make your final decision," J. D. Toole said.

The man wanted the prize of the showroom, a red Cadillac convertible with whitewall tires and matching interior. If Thelma were here, he told himself, she would have sold that man his Cadillac and a half-dozen shiny extras. J.D. knew he couldn't afford it. Thelma would have justified the sale by saying it's not her job to save the world, that if a grown man wants to buy a car, it's his responsibility to know whether or not he can afford it, not hers, and that commission money is for our family, and why should our child be denied what that money can provide because some man who should know what he's doing in the first place wants to buy a car. And who are you, John Dewey Toole, to judge whether or not this customer can afford that red Cadillac? He could be one of those eccentrics she'd heard about on television that had thousands of dollars hidden away under a floorboard and dressed like a bum but could buy the Taj Mahal. As his wife's imaginary tirade raged on in his head, what pained John Dewey Toole most was that this poor guy obviously had money at one time and probably could have afforded three of these Cadillacs. Everything about him spelled success except his current state. Something had happened, a messy divorce perhaps. This was a man trying to resurrect his spirit in the seat of a new car that would only bring him more misfortune, and John Dewey Toole was not going to be the salesman to do it.

All his life, J. D. Toole had prided himself on being an honorable man. He weighed each decision carefully. Doing what was right gave him joy. He measured his success differently than his peers, most of whom were driven by money and status, might. It was one of the reasons he didn't socialize. Perhaps his wife should have married someone more like those men, he often thought, and while he loved Thelma, he could see disappointment in her eyes, and the hard part was that the quality that disappointed her was what he liked most about himself, that he put others first. J. D. Toole chose his life and while he didn't regret it, not exactly, he did fear what was happening to him. He wasn't a fool. He knew these "episodes" were the harbinger of something serious. He recognized that he was becoming a caricature of himself. Just the other day a couple came into the dealership to purchase a Buick, not an expensive Cadillac or a top-of-the-line sports car, just an average, middle-class, affordable Buick. J.D. noticed the husband's loafers were scuffed, and twenty minutes into the deal, he had convinced himself if he sold the couple this car, they would become destitute, because if a man can't keep his shoes nice, then he must be negligent in both his personal and professional life, and if he's negligent in those areas, he'll eventually lose his job, and then he'll lose his wife, and then he won't be able to continue to afford this car.

As Kenny and his dad entered the kitchen, Thelma was humming "There's no business, like show business . . ." Kenny smiled. Sometimes she reminded him of Ethel Merman, bawdy, outspoken. A few of the kids at school made fun of

Kenny for liking performers like Merman, whom they considered ancients. He loved the glamour of Hollywood. He told himself that one day he would write about it.

"I didn't have time to cook," Thelma said. "Before you two sleeping beauties had even stirred, I ran to the bakery for fresh beignets." Thelma was in a good mood. She had just been hired by the local Rotary Club to put on a Christmas pageant and was ticking off her list as her husband and son hungrily began their breakfast. Kenny was a neat boy, but that warm, powdery doughnut was too delightful for him to eat carefully. He had to wash his hands twice to remove the sugar from his fingers. He had wanted to lick them clean but knew his mother wouldn't approve. As Thelma watched her son scrubbing his hands, her eyes glistened with pride that she had raised such a fastidious child.

"All ready for school, my darling?" Thelma asked.

Kenny nodded, pulling on his jacket. Thelma buttoned him up, giving him a tiny kiss on the cheek. "Do you know how much I love you?" she said. Kenny straightened his shoulders and proudly began reciting Elizabeth Barrett Browning's "How Do I Love Thee?"

"I love thee freely, as men strive for, for . . ." Kenny paused, searching for the word. "Wait, Mother, don't tell me."

Thelma smiled.

Kenny said: "It's light! I love thee freely, as men strive for light!"

"You're warm!" Thelma said.

"Strive for, I know, I know, flight, no, might!"

Kenny's forehead wrinkled in concentration. "Right!" he exclaimed. "I love thee freely as men strive for right!"

Kenny delighted in the Hot and Cold game, and he'd often play it with his mom. She'd hide something and as he would start searching, the only clues he would be given were hot, warm, or cold. They would play for hours. Sometimes it would be the words to a famous poem or sonnet written on a scrap of paper, other times she would hide tickets to a play or event that she knew her son would enjoy. The best prizes were books. Kenny loved to read and his mom encouraged his reverence for words. During their games, Thelma would hide books from Dr. Seuss and Rudyard Kipling to Mark Twain and L. Frank Baum. She wanted her son to appreciate literary voices. Though Thelma knew she was often thought tiresome, going on about her son's rare intelligence, she recognized long before his teachers that her Kenny had been blessed. "I love this child too much," Thelma would sometimes say to herself. Thelma rarely prayed at night, preferring to have her daily chat with God early in the mornings while her family was still sleeping. She didn't restrain herself when she needed something. She was as forthright with God as she was with everyone else. Her great fear, she would explain to him as she made her morning coffee, was her son dying before her. She realized this was an irrational concern, that Kenny was healthy and robust, and that she had taught him to look both ways before he crossed the street, to be careful and never to talk to strangers, not to get in a car with anyone he didn't know. She'd prepared him in every way that a mother could against peril and she had faith in his judgment. She chided herself for being upset if Kenny wanted to play outside with the neighborhood kids. Why shouldn't he, she thought? Thelma felt guilty for expecting so much from her son, but he had so much more to give the world than other children.

As winter cast its damp shadow across the Big Easy, Kenny focused on homework and assisting his mom with the Rotary Club Christmas pageant. He was excited to play Joseph in the Nativity skit. His mom ran his lines with him every day after school. When they were finished, if Dad was feeling okay, he would observe Kenny doing his arithmetic assignments. John Dewey enjoyed numbers and Kenny was a natural. Solving equations seemed to help J.D. stay in the present. During their study sessions, sometimes Kenny would notice his dad staring at the umbrella by the door and fixating on the dangers of its pointy tip or continually glancing back at the kitchen counter to make sure there were no knives left out, and he would wonder if he should be nervous about those things, too.

John Dewey Toole was determined that until lucidity fully abandoned him, he was going to be there for his family. He saw how pale his wife had become, her usual cherubic cheeks and broad smile dulled by lack of sleep. When it came to her Christmas pageants, Thelma was the consummate perfectionist, checking and rechecking every piece of sheet music, making sure all her handwritten notes were visible and clear, and that each young cast member would derive the proper amount of inspiration from her directives. On the nights that she wasn't rehearsing, she spent hours planning the choreography, making certain each performer was assigned numbers that best showcased their individual styles and personalities. She pored through sketches of set designs and prop lists trying to eliminate unnecessary expense, cursing the president of the club for such a paltry budget. Why couldn't he understand that an extravaganza featuring promising young talent whom she herself, Thelma Toole, had painstakingly nurtured and trained, and a timeless musical score and stunning stage decor that she personally chose all required substantial financial backing. She wondered if Michael Kidd, Jerome Robbins, or Busby Berkeley had to endure such constraints.

Thelma began jotting down notes for the event program. The Rotary Club had given her a limit on printing costs that required she not exceed one page. It was an impossible demand. She had so many people to recognize. The florists providing fresh flower arrangements who only acquiesced to Thelma's relentless campaign upon the promise they'd be prominently acknowledged in the program. The bakery delivering warm holiday cookies and coffee for the intermission, the deli making the snack packs for the kids backstage, the moms volunteering to help with makeup and hair, the printer to whom Thelma offered a discount on his son's elocution lessons, the hardware store that donated paint, the janitor who volunteered to be a stagehand and manage set changes, the photographer, the piano tuner, the cleanup crew, and a dozen other people whom Thelma had kept pestering with letters, phone calls, and carefully timed visits until they couldn't say no. At least she didn't have to worry about the tailor anymore. He'd politely withdrawn after she brought over twenty-nine costumes with detailed instructions pinned to each one. Good Christ, he thought, the Rockettes were less work.

The holidays flew by and as the weeks turned into months and the seasons blended one into the next, Kenny began to experience the stirrings of puberty. The chubby little boy whom the other kids teased and called fat started to grow long and lean. His voice deepened and his chin was showing signs of stubble. On a Saturday morning during his sophomore year, Thelma caught her son attempting to shave with his dad's straight razor. He was concentrating so hard that he didn't notice his mom standing there observing him. Normally Thelma would have scolded him for not asking permission, but something about the way Kenny gingerly handled the razor, his careful calculation, his determination to master this manly ritual on his own, made her proud.

As his body matured, so too did Kenny's curiosity about girls. In junior year, the all-boys high school he attended became coed, and like most of his male classmates, Kenny found himself bewitched and bewildered. It seemed everywhere he turned his senses were assailed by images of supple flesh, delicate curves, and the scent of fresh soap and strawberry lip gloss. Kenny had never talked about sex with his parents. It was too embarrassing to discuss with his mom and when Kenny asked his dad, he mumbled something to his son about how important it was to stay clean down there. Kenny tried to cope with puberty on his own, reading the encyclopedia after his parents went to sleep to try and understand what was happening to him. There were nights he'd awaken ashamed. He'd hurry into the bathroom and douse a washcloth in cold water, dabbing at the stains on his sheets until they were gone. He finally called his uncle Arthur, who reassured his nephew that it was a normal, healthy part of growing up.

Uncle Arthur, Thelma's brother, had always been like a second father to Kenny. A petite Southern gentleman with a generous spirit and smart sense of humor, he saw a lot of himself in his precocious nephew. The other day, he had taken Kenny out for ice cream. While they were enjoying double scoops of vanilla in sugary waffle cones, Arthur noticed that Kenny was withdrawn, barely eating his ice cream. Arthur understood that pushing Kenny to open up, when his mother already pushed him too hard, would only make him retreat more. As they were leaving the ice cream parlor, Kenny was fighting back tears.

"Kid, what it is it?" Arthur asked.

"Can I live with you?"

Arthur wanted to head straight to Webster Street and pack his nephew's belongings. He knew things were hard at home and he was worried about Kenny. Arthur also realized that Kenny was his sister's whole world and if she ever found out Kenny had asked to live with him, it would wound her. Arthur hugged his nephew and explained how it wouldn't be fair to his mom and dad, who loved him and needed him to be strong right now. Then he drove him back to Webster Street. Twice he wanted to turn around but didn't.

Kenny experienced his first crush early in his senior year. She was a girl in his English class. Petite with auburn hair and the most beautiful green eyes, if glitter had a sound, that's what her laugh reminded him of. He was so nervous around her that he'd blush self-consciously and fumble for words. One afternoon a group of Kenny's classmates snickered when the teacher asked him a question about *The Canterbury Tales* and he was tongue-tied. Kenny had done his homework on Chaucer but he couldn't concentrate when she sat one desk in front of him. She was two years older. Being the youngest senior was a burden he carried silently. He acted the part of the class clown, pretending it didn't bother him, but there were days he came home from school wishing he never had to go back.

"Mr. Toole!" the teacher said. "I'm waiting . . ."

"I'm sorry, sir," Kenny replied. He thought about how disappointed his mother would be if she were here witnessing him humiliating himself. "What was the question again?"

Before his teacher could repeat it, the bell rang. Kenny gathered his books and began making his way to his next class, dreaming of the auburn-haired girl and what it might be like to kiss her. When he got home from school, his mom had a snack waiting on the kitchen counter with a note letting him know that she was teaching music lessons this evening. He said hello to his dad, then went to his room and locked the door. One good thing about his dad's constantly changing the locks, when Kenny asked him to have a lock on his bedroom door, his dad was impressed that his son appreciated the value of security. Thelma was furious, believing it inappropriate for an adolescent to be able to lock out his parents. What if he had an accident and she couldn't get in his room in time to save him?

Kenny closed and locked his door. Then he took out his favorite composition book from its hiding place and his lucky fountain pen that his uncle Arthur gave him for his birthday, lucky because it produced an A in every essay at school, and he began to write. Kenny loved the sound of the pen moving across the paper, the music of his escape from the world. Sometimes when he wrote, he closed his eyes, setting free the thoughts that were burning inside his brain where they could have a life of their own, free from judgment or criticism.

As the writing lifted him to his secret place, he felt his desire for the auburn-haired girl guiding his pen, transforming his prose into an impassioned letter to her. He promised to love and cherish her forever. He quoted Emily Dickinson. He introduced scenes from his favorite movies. Kenny filled page after page in an earnest declaration of his affection. He would have kept on if it wasn't for his mother announcing that dinner would be ready in five minutes. Kenny wiped his lucky pen with a felt cloth and carefully placed it back in its velvet box. Then he closed his composition book and returned it to its hiding place.

Thelma wasn't herself at dinner. She barely ate and kept folding and refolding her napkin, staring at the curio cabinet. "How on earth am I going to pack all that crystal properly in time for the movers?" she said.

"Mom, what are you talking about?"

"I'm sorry, darling, but your father isn't making any commissions and I can't keep up with the bills here. I've found us a lovely apartment on Cambronne Street and it'll be more convenient because it's closer to your school."

Kenny shifted uncomfortably in his chair, wishing he could be anywhere but in that dining room with his mother, feeling as if they both had the weight of the world on their shoulders.

In the weeks that followed, the Tooles packed up their lives and moved, leaving behind the affluent neighborhood that Thelma coveted. Kenny could tell his mom was withering like those gardenias he sometimes saw in people's front yards that weren't getting enough sunlight. They still smelled sweet but it was as if they were folding in on themselves and no longer wished to be flowers. As the movers delivered the last of the Tooles' boxes to the new apartment, a friend of Kenny's from school invited him to spend a few days at his aunt and uncle's farm in rural Mississippi. Kenny didn't feel right abandoning his parents, but on the morning of the trip, Thelma hugged her son, handed him a box of fresh pralines, and lovingly scooted him out the door, whispering to have a wonderful time and to remember to mind his manners. As she watched Kenny walk away, she gripped the tiny St. Christopher medal that she always kept in her pocket. It was going to be a long night. Since they'd arrived at Cambronne Street, her husband would open one box and then another, pull a few things out of each, and then stack the unpacked boxes in the back alley to be discarded. Thelma had to rescue their belongings, carrying the items back into the house. The building superintendent, seeing her struggling, gave her a shopping cart. By the time she'd retrieved the last load, Thelma had never felt wearier. She cried softly, grateful her son was far away. "Stop it!" she told herself. The sun was beginning to set, bathing the room in warm shades of gold and peach. She closed her eyes, envisioning Kenny entertaining everyone, or perhaps he was riding a tractor or playing hide-and-seek in the cornfields. The image of her child in the clean country air comforted her. Shaking off her sadness, she stood up, smoothed down her housedress, and began emptying the shopping cart.

Kenny's visit to Mississippi felt like a dream. Though he would never tell his mother this, he wished they could live on a farm. Boys only had to wear ties if they were going to church, a wedding, or a funeral. His friend's cousins had everyday clothes and Sunday clothes, and they could get their everyday clothes as dirty as they liked and no one would care. Late one night, long past his curfew at home, his friend handed him a Ball jar with a lid. They went outside and Kenny caught his first firefly. They whooped and hollered in delight as Kenny watched the panicked creature desperately try to find a way out, fluttering its wings against the glass. He opened his jar and set it free.

On the trip back to New Orleans, Kenny became fascinated by the billboards. Every time he looked up there was one warning sinners about the fires of hell and eternal damnation. Kenny didn't think much about hell except when he went exploring in the French Quarter and saw people who lived on the streets begging for food. His mom had told him that they were lost souls and to pray for them. Kenny wondered, if those people went to the places advertised on the billboards, would they find their souls or at least something to eat? When he got home, Thelma was waiting by the doorway. She handed him an envelope from his school.

"Aren't you going to open it?"

The envelope felt moist and when Kenny inserted his thumbnail underneath the front flap, it lifted a little too easily. He pulled out the letter that was inside, noticing a faint smudge in the upper right-hand corner.

"Come on, read me what it says," Thelma said.

Kenny swallowed back his annoyance and read the letter. It said he had won a tour of Washington, DC; New York City; and Philadelphia for his exemplary academic performance. He would depart in early May, before graduation. Thelma clapped, delighted for her son. She had already begun saving the money to buy Kenny a new suit for the trip.

The school year moved quickly and Kenny continued to think about the auburn-haired girl. He'd finally mustered the courage to introduce himself as his mom had taught him, addressing her by her last name. She told him to call her Ginny, short for Virginia. Once in a while after English period they'd talk by the lockers. That afternoon she told him that she liked the way he could always make her smile.

As the May trip neared, Kenny became more excited. He was disappointed Ginny wouldn't be going but busied himself reading about the history of each of the three cities he'd be visiting. He was especially curious about New York. On the day of departure, Thelma handed him a fifty-dollar bill and told him to buy something special. He knew how hard his mother had to work for that fifty dollars.

Many years later, he would embark on a similar sojourn that would also see him cross several state lines, but that departure would be marked by the slamming of a door and screeching tires. Neither mother nor son knew any of that then. If they had, perhaps, they would have held on to each other just a moment more when they said goodbye on that bright, hopeful spring morning.

⎯⎯⎯

No one knew that Kenny had written his first novel except his uncle Arthur, whom he had to confide in because he put his address on the submission form. He didn't want to risk his mother finding out about the contest. She would put all her hopes and dreams on his winning, and he wasn't ready for that, not yet.

Kenny had heard about the competition from the school librarian. A kindhearted man who reminded Kenny of his dad, he was walking past the cafeteria one afternoon and saw the way some of the older boys treated Kenny. He'd let Kenny eat lunch in the library ever since. When Kenny asked him why he was given that privilege, he told him he wanted to encourage his love for reading. Kenny chose the title *The Neon Bible* for his novel, one of the billboards he had seen in

Mississippi. The story was about a young boy who had to do a terrible thing for the right reasons.

The librarian told him that the best writers drew upon their own personal experience. He took his advice to heart. That was the other reason he didn't want his mom to know about it. The character of Aunt Mae was a lot like her but she was a caricature. Kenny was learning about caricatures in art class, and he realized, if someone can draw a caricature with pictures, why couldn't he create one using words instead? The family featured in the story had to move from a good neighborhood to one that wasn't so nice, and it caused suffering. Kenny was afraid if his mom read that, she would believe he had suffered because of their move downtown. Kenny worked tirelessly, filling composition book after composition book, writing and rewriting. He wrote after his parents were in bed, during the day in the library, and anywhere else he could lose himself in his characters without being seen. When he was finished, his novel was thirty pages. He'd written it with his lucky fountain pen.

As soon as he returned from his class trip, he couldn't wait to call his uncle Arthur to see if the letter containing the results from the contest had arrived. He didn't want to call him until his mom was out of the house. Finally, he dialed the phone.

"Hi, Kenny," his uncle said.

"It is there?"

"Yes sirree, I'm holding the envelope in my hand."

"Okay, on the count of three, I want you to open it."

Kenny could hear the tearing of paper.

Silence.

"Uncle Arthur?"

"Kenny, I'm afraid it's not the news we were hoping for . . ."

That night, Kenny took his lucky fountain pen and stuffed it angrily in the back of his closet, vowing never to use it again.

FOUR

---⟋⟍⟋⟍---

Sixteen-year-old Kenny Toole was shaking his head as he listened to his mother complain about the boxes cluttering the foyer of their new apartment. Good Lord, he thought, as he filled out the last of the change of address cards, is she never satisfied? They'd packed all their belongings and moved to Audubon Street before the old lease had even expired. Kenny's dad was so confused that he couldn't remember which address he now lived at. A policeman noticed him standing at an intersection. When the policeman approached J.D., something about the man seemed familiar to him. The man looked so frail and thin but the policeman couldn't shake the feeling that they'd met before, and then, suddenly, he remembered. This was the salesman who had sold him and his wife their first automobile several years earlier. It was a baby blue station wagon, a beauty. The policeman remembered how kind he had been, how he had talked the couple out of a Corvette and thank God he had, because not soon after, he and the Mrs. discovered they were expecting. The policeman guided him back to the curb and drove him home, relieved that he knew his address. J.D. thanked him and got out of the car.

The year is 1954. As Frank Sinatra and Tony Bennett are making ladies swoon over the radio and Marlon Brando is redefining the masculine ideal in *On the Waterfront*, the future king of rock and roll, a bedroom-eyed Southern boy, cuts his first commercial recording in Memphis, Tennessee. Dwight D. Eisenhower is president and more women are joining the workforce, shedding the role of homemaker to embrace identities of their own.

Kenny didn't mind living on Cambronne Street, but Thelma was miserable and couldn't adjust to a neighborhood where no one, she insisted, could appreciate Longfellow or Fitzgerald, if they even knew who they were. Though Kenny never said it out loud, he feared his mother was a snob. When he was little, she'd go on and on about her Creole heritage and about how her ancestors were among Louisiana's elite or some such prattle, but to Kenny, none of it mattered. A family tree or a last name didn't make a man. Although Kenny enjoyed the idea of hobnobbing with the "right people," Thelma's pursuit of this elusive ideal was exhausting. He was already working odd jobs to help pay for the increase in rent, swinging a full course load at Tulane, and taking care of his dad. Since the incident with the policeman, Thelma had taken J.D. to several specialists hoping for answers. The doctors hadn't been much help, saying that confusion was common after sixty. He still dressed himself and could carry on a conversation if whoever he was talking with continually reminded him what the subject was. The dealership was pushing for him to retire but Thelma begged them to let her husband stay. "It'll kill him if he can't come here," she had explained. "What else does he have?" They reluctantly acquiesced, but that just meant more burden on Kenny, who often had to fetch his dad from the showroom because he couldn't recall why he was there.

The new apartment did have its perks. Kenny could walk to Tulane. During those precious moments alone, he would soak in the sounds and scents of this idyllic, Southern hamlet, the rustling of leaves, a bird calling its mate, the occasional toot of a horn, the heady fragrance of jasmine, the colorful bougainvillea. His mind free of the oppressive hum of discontent on Audubon Street, Kenny would skip to campus sometimes, his feet as light as his spirit as he anticipated a future that he was certain would include wonderful strolls like this, but instead of returning to a household where broken dreams stank like spiled milk that had soaked into the floorboards, its sour stench lingering in the halls, Kenny vowed that his own home would always be fresh. There would be no unresolved discontent to spoil the pure air on his manicured porch or the rich mahogany smell of his elegant study, where he would showcase his rare book collection in custom-built shelves and where his son would sit on his lap and ask him to read a story, perhaps

Peter Rabbit, though if it was his daughter, he would insist on *Winnie-the-Pooh*, because he remembered how frightened he had been for Peter Rabbit when he was a child, and wouldn't want his daughter to have nightmares. Kenny often thought about fatherhood. The sixteen-year-old Kenny was going to choose his wife carefully. This decision would require clear thinking, courage, and above all truthfulness with oneself. He would not pick the prettiest woman because that could be trouble. No, he would pick the worthiest one, the woman who would love him in all the ways his mother couldn't love his father.

Kenny wondered if Ginny the auburn-haired girl would make a suitable wife. While they had gone out on several dates, she hadn't understood why Thelma always accompanied them. She had longed for Kenny to be her first kiss, but she finally had to let another boy do the honors, as Kenny wouldn't kiss her with his mom surveilling them. She remembered once, after they had seen *Rear Window* at the movies, she had been frightened for Grace Kelly and grabbed Kenny's hand and squeezed it. She was sure he'd kiss her that night and when Thelma went to powder her nose Kenny leaned into her and he was going to do it, but then Thelma reappeared, saying she'd forgotten her handbag. Ginny knew she hadn't forgotten it.

Though Kenny missed Ginny, between taking her out and having to pay for his mom, too, the cost of school books and supplies, and helping his parents, he had been working more hours than his body could endure. There were days he would go without sleep, and when depression creeped up, he would push the monster back into a box in his brain and pretend to forget it was there, growing and growling, determined that one day it would escape and devour the boy who put it inside.

Kenny's sanctuary was college. In class, listening to his professors, Kenny was lifted from the doldrums of his life to the possibilities of what it could be. He briefly thought about majoring in engineering, but after braving a handful of lectures during which he kept looking at the clock, praying there'd be a fire drill, Kenny realized that he had to follow his calling, and it wasn't mathematics or blueprints, it was the written word, the power of a writer to create an entire world with their imagination, to make people feel and think, to challenge the lens through which they saw themselves. Kenny remembered hearing somewhere that the definition of a good book was that you missed the characters after you finished reading it. He thought it the finest measurement of a gifted writer that he'd ever heard. He tried to do that with *The Neon Bible*. For him, the characters were as real as his own family, in fact, they *were* his family while he was writing it and for a long time after. When that stupid form letter arrived telling him to try again next year, he'd felt as if someone had killed his loved ones and buried them in a potter's field without so much as a gravestone marking their memory.

The semesters at Tulane flew by. During the summers, Kenny would take trips with school friends. One of his buddies had an old DeSoto. He, Kenny, and another classmate would cruise to the beach in Biloxi, enjoying the surf and flirting with girls, or they'd go on road trips. His favorite was their visit to New York City. Kenny had been wanting to return there without a chaperone or curfews, so on a hot July morning in 1956, they headed in the direction of Manhattan. They shared paying for gas and turns at the wheel. When they needed a break, they'd park somewhere and nap. They made it in two days, passing the time discussing literature and art, baseball and cars, and debating the merits of large breasts. They dined at all-you-can-eat roadside restaurants, stuffing themselves. One of the boys, a business major who fancied himself a sea-food connoisseur, devoured three servings of fried catfish, and when he ordered more, the manager came to the table asking if this was some sort of joke.

"No," he replied. "Traveling makes me hungry."

The man went to the kitchen and came back with a bucket full of entrails and fish heads. *"Bon appetit!"*

The rest of the drive, Kenny mimicked the restaurant pro-prietor, making his friends laugh so hard they had to pull over. Kenny and his cohorts arrived in New York at dawn. As they wound their way down FDR Drive, mesmerized by the East River glistening in the sun, the magnificent buildings stretching toward the heavens, the bright yellow taxi cabs signaling the start of the early morning rush, they were silent, each lost in his own thoughts. By the time they reached the Y, the promise of adventure had washed away the need for sleep. After they settled in, they donned the smart clothes each brought along at the insistence of their mothers. One of the boys grabbed the car keys. Kenny explained that in New York, people got around by subway. The business major looked alarmed.

"My mom told me never to go down there," he said. "There might be prostitutes."

Kenny burst into an interpretation of a frightened, overly protective mother, his voice reaching to a crescendo, his hands gesturing wildly. He then herded them out.

Kenny's comrades dutifully followed him. As they waited for the subway, Kenny imagined what it would be like to live in New York. He envisioned being a famous writer with a lavish apartment overlooking Central Park and a British manservant that would make sure his ties were always pressed and his shirts were properly starched. Kenny would learn how to cook coq au vin, which he was certain would make the girls swoon. He would have a giant blackboard in his bedroom so that when inspiration called in the wee hours, he could take a piece of yellow chalk and indulge himself with large, sweeping strokes across that marvelous flat surface. After he'd filled the blackboard just as he did his composition books, he would go back to bed, and when he woke up, he could admire his work as he had done when he was in elementary school and his teacher let him draw on the blackboard instead of going outside for recess.

Kenny's school chums were impressed by how easily he navigated the city, taking them to storied locations and regaling them with tales of the denizens who had left their indelible imprint. Their first stop that afternoon was the White Horse Tavern in Greenwich Village. Kenny had read all about the famed establishment. Built in 1880, it was originally a pub for longshoremen and over the years had become a gathering place for writers and artists. Kenny was so excited by the ambiance and history that he already knew what he would drink in honor of one of his literary heroes. Kenny remembered reading Dylan Thomas's obituary two years earlier, that he had died after a night of boozing at the White Horse. He was only thirty-nine years old. When Kenny heard about this brilliant writer's demise, he was struck by the irony that a man with so much to live for would be extinguished so soon.

Next, the boys decided on Carnegie Hall. It was a beautiful day, unseasonably cool for New York in July, so they walked. Kenny pointed out landmarks along the way, explaining their significance. He enjoyed playing tour guide and would burst into character for some of his orations. As they approached 42nd Street, with its mix of art-house and commercial movie theaters, Kenny changed his gait from long, casual strides to short, determined steps. He tousled his hair, letting some of it fall across his forehead, smiled until his eyebrows crinkled, and then, relaxing his belly so that it protruded over his belt, imitated the great Mayor Fiorello La Guardia in his booming New York–Italian voice, delighting his friends with the history of Hell's Kitchen. Their friend was making this trip even better than anticipated. With Kenny, there was always laughter. He had a way of looking at the world that inspired them.

They stopped at a newsstand and Kenny purchased a copy of the *Daily News*, flipping through the movie listings. He noticed that an art house on the block was showing an Ingmar Bergman film and if they hustled, they could still make the matinee. Kenny had never seen the Swedish filmmaker's work but he'd read about the man's unbounded genius. When

Kenny told his friends that they were seeing a Bergman film, one of them said he loved her in *Casablanc*a. By the time the boys got there, they were several minutes late. The entrance was cramped right next to an adjacent theater. They rushed to the ticket counter, paid their money and entered the vestibule.

Ninety minutes later they exited. Stunned.

It was not what Kenny had expected and not the extravagant talent that he had promised his friends they would witness. The film was decidedly odd and the characters seemed to be talking in Japanese. Unbeknownst to them, they had gone into the wrong theater. The movie they had seen was *Godzilla*. The film directed by Mr. Bergman was next door.

The sun was beginning to set as the boys continued their trek north. When they reached Carnegie Hall, Kenny stared at the building, envisioning the great performers who had graced its stage. He thought of his mother and how she would have loved sharing this moment with him. He felt guilty for not checking in, but long-distance phone calls weren't in the budget and he didn't want to think about home. All he cared about right now was squeezing in every bit of goodness that he could from this trip, like the food from those roadside diners. He dashed inside a gift shop, bought a postcard, and then rejoined his friends.

They had one more adventure to conclude their day. Kenny had always been curious about the Russian Tea Room. He convinced his companions it would be worth seeing but they didn't have enough money for all three so they flipped a coin. Whoever won would eat modestly and report to the others.

Kenny and the business major lost the coin toss. The winner was raised in rural Louisiana on the bayou. Kenny told him a little bit about the history of the Tea Room, that he had seen pictures of the inside and it reminded him of something out of a Hans Christian Andersen fairytale. After Kenny and the other boy left the lucky winner at the entrance, reminding him that they expected details, they decided to explore the atrium at the Plaza Hotel. When the maître d' of the lobby bar saw them lingering and asked if they'd like a table, they both nodded.

Kenny's friend: "This place looks kind of expensive."

Kenny: "We'll just order one drink apiece."

They consulted the menu.

"We'll have two glasses of ice cold water with fresh lemon," Kenny informed the waiter.

As they sipped their drinks, admiring the richly dressed patrons and the buzz of people chatting over cocktails, the waiter returned placing a billfold on the table.

"We only had water!" Kenny's friend whispered.

Kenny retrieved the neatly tucked bill from its leather folio. He grew pale.

"What is it?" his friend asked.

"A lesson."

The surcharge for the table was almost equal to the tab at the White Horse. Kenny briefly considered the ole dine and dash because they didn't really dine after all, and tap water was supposed to be free, but he thought of his father and how that would disappoint him so he anted up. As the two boys were leaving the Plaza, she walked in. His Uncle Arthur couldn't understand how he could have a crush on an actress who played a boy on Broadway, but Kenny thought she was the prettiest thing in the world. He'd seen Mary Martin on TV and decided right there and then, standing in the foyer of the Plaza, that television didn't do a person justice. He wanted to ask the impish beauty for her autograph but she moved with quick, purposeful steps as if she were meeting someone and didn't want to be late. He wondered if it was a lover and he felt a twinge of jealousy. She was getting nearer. He held his breath, fumbling for the courage to speak. Just then the star smiled at him as she passed and winked.

"Do you know her?" his friend asked.

Kenny didn't answer, wanting this moment all to himself.

As the two boys arrived at the Russian Tea Room, their companion was already outside waiting for them. He didn't look well.

"I ordered borscht because I'd heard of it," he said. "It's the worst thing I ever tasted in my entire life! I didn't want to get their fancy napkin dirty so I went into the bathroom to spit it out."

Kenny could tell that he was embarrassed and so announced he would have done exactly the same. For a second, an image of Thelma looking at him disapprovingly flashed through his mind.

"Hey guys, I'm starving," Kenny said. "Let's go to that diner next to the Y and get some burgers." As they walked to the subway, Kenny knew that it was only a matter of time before this city beckoned to him again. He belonged here with all the other artists and dreamers who left the familiar environs of home to realize their destiny. Kenny wasn't sure how he'd break the news to his parents. He wasn't even certain how he'd be able to afford New York. He had nothing except for a dream and the promise he made to himself that night that one day his name would mean something in this town. The decision made, now the plan. Kenny closed his eyes and imagined what the philosopher Boethius, whose works were among Kenny's favorite indulgences, would tell him to do. A half hour later, as Kenny and his friends were savoring their burgers, reliving their hijinks of the afternoon, he felt a determination swelling within him.

The rest of their visit to New York was a blur. They squeezed in everything from male-only clubs in the East Village and window shopping at Macy's on 34th Street to a stroll through Central Park and playing tambourines with a disheveled group of beatniks in Washington Square Park. One of them asked Kenny if he'd like to get high. Kenny had never smoked pot before. He gingerly put the joint in his mouth and took a few tokes. Not entirely unpleasant, he thought. It was their last morning, and the boys decided to make a stop at the Museum of Modern Art. When they arrived, they showed the clerk their student IDs, paid fifty cents apiece, and walked inside. The museum was featuring Jackson Pollock. Kenny had heard about Pollock but had little interest in his work. He liked artists such as Caravaggio and Rembrandt whom he'd learned about his first year at Tulane. Their paintings were so lifelike Kenny felt if he talked to them they would answer. He'd heard about Pollock's technique, how he'd lain a large canvas on the floor of his studio in East Hampton. Kenny had thought he'd just dribbled the paint, but up close it looked more like he lashed the paint onto the canvas, bending over, walking around, attacking it from all sides. In the end, it had the uniformity of a piece complete. This was a different kind of art, a different kind of painting. Mostly, Kenny thought painters looked out over their canvas and painted what they saw in the world. Pollock looked down and painted what came from deep inside himself. It was raw, beautiful, transfixing. Kenny surprised himself. He understood this clearly. It's what he'd want to do if he were a painter.

The drive to New Orleans was pleasant and the conversation lively. They stopped at one of the same roadside restaurants. The waitress remembered the three college boys. She couldn't help but notice that the handsome one who made everybody laugh when they were first here seemed reserved, older somehow. He smiled but didn't talk much.

FIVE

———

Graduate student Kenny Toole was sitting on the library steps at Columbia University, hunched over, engrossed in a book that he felt guilty indulging in because there were so many others he should have been reading for class. The author had him by the shoulders and was shaking Kenny awake from a meaningless slumber in which professors and critics droned on about almost nothing, where here in the pages of this hedonistic tome he felt alive. Kenny had heard somewhere that the book had been written on one long continuous scroll of parchment whose truth couldn't be restrained any more than the anger inside the soul of its creator. Kenny had done some research on the man and learned that his mom had been overbearing and probably relished that her son kept running back home to her when life was doling out more than he could handle. The author's mother was his leash and collar, and the only time he seemed free of her was when he was writing. Kenny understood. Thelma was a thousand miles away yet he could sense her breath on his neck, willing him to excel and mind his manners, make her proud.

As he strolled to class, his mind drifted to Ginny. He wondered if she had ever married. The last time he saw her, that night at the movie theater, he had wanted so badly to kiss her, but then Thelma had walked in, stifling his nerve, and he knew he'd probably never see her again. He'd thought about inviting her to visit him in New York, but every time he started writing, he was uncertain of what to say. New York girls were intimidating. He'd met some of the girls from Barnard and there were a few he thought about asking out, but something always stopped him. Perhaps it was the way they allowed themselves to be who they were. They offered their opinions, often loudly, on matters from politics and art to economics and sex. They didn't seem to care what anyone thought, anathema to the demurring nature of most Southern girls, and Kenny was attracted to the bawdiest and most outspoken of the lot. Whenever he attempted a romantic gesture, he experienced an annoying thumping in his chest prompting the girl to inquire if he was feeling okay.

There was this one girl. She was a freshman and wanted his opinion on declaring a major. She was thinking literature because she had fallen in love with Rimbaud and Chatterton and was happiest losing herself in their words, but her parents were set on her pursuing a career in medicine. Her grandfather and father were both surgeons and she would be the first female doctor in the family. She still hadn't told them she wanted to become a writer. When she met Kenny, she felt he understood. He saw something in her that no one else did, and he made her believe there was nothing she couldn't achieve. They met at a diner near campus. She was cramming for midterms and Kenny could tell by the way she kept rubbing her forehead that she was overwhelmed. He asked if he could help.

"I don't know," she said. "Are you any good at anatomy?"

"No, but I'm very good at taking tests," Kenny replied. "I can show you some tricks to help you memorize this stuff in no time."

"My name is Ellen," she said, extending her hand.

She was hoping he'd ask her up to his room to study. He was so handsome and his Southern accent was maybe the dreamiest thing she'd ever heard.

Kenny did something he never did that day. He missed class.

The year is 1958. The Hula-Hoop debuts and one hundred million are sold. *Gigi* wins nine Oscars while Alfred Hitchcock's *Vertigo* disappoints both moviegoers and film critics. The microchip is invented, NASA is born, and the first US passenger jets paint lines of white across the sky. The postwar optimism that inspired the baby boom is cowering under rising unemployment and a recession. For a younger generation, the *Howl* of discontent looms.

As his first semester at Columbia progressed, Kenny inhaled the energy of New York, breathing it in as deeply as he could, desperate to convince himself that this was where he belonged. He missed the institutions of the South, the genteel manners, the way in which people always said sir and ma'am and knew what a proper thank-you was. Back home, a man had time to think, to appreciate someone's garden or linger at the doorway of a bakery. In New York, Kenny would grab a bagel and eat it as he rushed to class, hardly tasting it. Kenny was frantically trying to complete his master's by summer. Most students took a year and a half to two years to get it done. Kenny had permitted himself ten months. It was the only financial possibility. Every morning, Kenny was up hours before his roommates. He slept fitfully, often waking as if from a nightmare, his head buzzing with everything he had to accomplish. He started keeping a notepad and some crayons from the box his dad had given him one Christmas on his nightstand, so if he woke up unable to shut his mind off, he'd write his thoughts down. Kenny had filled three notebooks already, and worn most of the crayons to nubs.

His biggest challenge was his master's thesis. He'd written a paper at Tulane that might suffice with a few adjustments and a new introduction. He didn't like himself for considering it but if he started fresh, he'd never make his deadline. Even though it wasn't technically cheating, the university would frown upon it and, if his dad found out, it would disappoint him. Kenny believed that somewhere inside of his father, there was still the parent who never let him take the easy way out as a boy and wouldn't like him doing it as a man.

Distraught, needing to escape this worrisome subject, Kenny decided the Village might offer respite. He had heard Beats on campus talking about a place on MacDougal that was diverting. Kenny felt like walking. It was mid-November, the air was brisk, and Manhattan was at its most alive. He made his way down Broadway to Columbus Circle, where he took a train to the Village. It was early evening as he came out of the subway and the sun had begun to set. As he walked toward MacDougal he was aware of the sounds around him, a street musician playing bongos made out of garbage can lids, a dog barking, cars honking, a philosopher pontificating, all of them competing to be heard. He closed his eyes and imagined he was back in the French Quarter, wanting to feel, if only for a moment, a connection to home. Both cities were loud, he concluded, but New Orleans had an optimism in its voice, a playfulness beneath the hum and clatter. New York didn't, he thought. If what a place sounded like could be a color, Kenny decided he'd choose red, like his mama's favorite lipstick, for New Orleans, the one she only wore on special occasions, and brown for New York, the same shade as his dad's slippers that he refused to part with, despite being faded and stained, because they were comfortable. Kenny wanted to feel comfortable in New York. He practiced being a New Yorker. He mastered the art of eating a slice of pizza the way New Yorkers did, folding it like a tortilla. He didn't spill sauce on his shirt anymore. He learned to like knishes, though they could never compare to a hot, fragrant beignet. He moved quickly and efficiently wherever he went, his senses alert, his gait determined. He also added more accessories to his wardrobe. He couldn't afford new clothes, but it was thrilling what a scarf or a hat could do. He also became a dedicated Yankees fan and could recite Mickey Mantle's latest heroics on or off the field. Soon, Kenny said to himself, New York will feel more like home than New Orleans. Having calmed his anxiety, he searched for the Gaslight. He nearly walked past it. It looked like an entrance to a run-down basement apartment. There were several steps leading to a dark, dingy doorway. Kenny could hear commotion on the other side. He opened the door and went in. It took him a moment to adjust to the dark and identify an empty table. The denizens were mostly male. Their clothes made him think of uniforms, dark colors, a little too big, and lived in. He located a table with an empty chair. He noticed a young woman also sitting there. She waved him down. He gave her a polite nod before sitting. She was young, wearing a Boston University sweatshirt.

He said to her, "I only had to travel down from 112th Street, but you came all the way from Boston?"

"I'm visiting some friends," she said. "They told me I should check out the scene here."

"Are you a musician?" he asked.

"I sing," she replied. "I like telling stories."

"I like telling stories, too," Kenny said. "I'm going to be a writer." This was the first time he'd said those words out loud and it felt good.

"What do you write about?"

"I've been playing with this idea of a novel about New Orleans."

"Is that where you're from?"

"Yes, and there are so many stories there no one sees. The eccentric old man selling hotdogs on Bourbon Street who probably sleeps in the street, the middle-aged stripper alone at the corner of the bar wishing she was young again, drinking herself numb, the tired-looking cop working the Quarter. I want to give them a voice."

"I know what you mean," she said. "I've been thinking about writing my own songs. It's about living your truth. Who knows, maybe one day I'll be on the radio and your book will be reviewed by the *New York Times*."

Kenny was intrigued. This girl couldn't have been more than seventeen years old yet it felt like he was talking to an old soul camouflaged in the body of a coed. She had a worldliness about her that didn't come from books or professors. Her voice was soft and melodic, a stark contrast to her dark brown eyes that danced with mischief.

"I wrote a novel before," Kenny said. "It was for a contest. A long time ago. I didn't win."

He wasn't like anyone she'd ever met. He was an old-fashioned gentleman. He reminded her of the characters in the hundred-year-old ballads she loved to sing. She thought, Perhaps one day, I'll write a song about him. He seemed so out of place to her in his tailored chinos, freshly starched shirt, and blazer.

"What's your name?" she asked.

"John Toole," he replied.

"I'm Joanie," she said, shaking his hand.

Before they could chat further, the house lights dimmed and someone ascended the stage. Skinny with long hair and a beard and dressed in loose fitting dungarees and what appeared to be a Native American vest, he pulled the microphone in close, and began reciting some sort of poem. Joanie was listening intently and Kenny didn't want her to think that he didn't appreciate rougher poetry. Every once in a while, the man would stop for a long pregnant pause, as if he were waiting for the importance of what he'd just said to sink in. Kenny watched him surveying his audience hopefully, as if he were expecting radiant beams to start shooting out of their heads, his words transforming the dank little room into an orgy of enlightenment. Kenny dug his thumbnail into his palm to keep from laughing. Then, everyone began snapping their fingers. Kenny was never good at snapping. He remembered when he was in kindergarten, the kids teasing him because whenever he tried, no sound would come out. J.D. spent weeks trying to show his son how to execute a proper snap. Kenny concentrated hard, attempting to recall exactly how his father had shown him to do it and gave it a few tries. Much to his relief, the snapping stopped as another poet took the stage.

Joanie explained that the reason everyone snapped their fingers was because the windows of the Gaslight opened into the air shafts, and when people applauded, the neighbors sometimes called the police, so the audience started snapping instead. Kenny was impressed. Then someone handed

Kenny a basket. He looked at Joanie, not quite certain what was expected.

"It's just like church," she said.

Kenny put a dollar in the basket and passed it to the next table.

Kenny offered to walk Joanie home but her friends were meeting her at a bar next door, purported to have the best charcoal-grilled burgers in the Village, she told him. She invited him to join her, but Kenny had an early class and he had already stayed out much too late. They walked outside together. Joanie sang a song for Kenny right there standing on the sidewalk, a lovely ballad about a girl named Flora who betrayed her lover and how it drove him to do something awful. It made Kenny think of David from *The Neon Bible* and how he had to do something awful, too. Kenny listened to Joanie sing, thinking perhaps his story wasn't that bad after all, that maybe if he gave it to her, she could make a song out of it like the one she was singing. He meant to get her number but before he could, she saw her friends arriving, kissed him on the cheek, and dashed off. He thought about Joanie the whole train ride home.

Kenny returned to New Orleans for the holidays. Thelma kept asking him his plans for the future. He carefully avoided the conversation.

Thelma saw a change in her son. He wasn't as polite, she thought. What decent boy walks away from a discussion with his mother? She chalked up his moodiness to the idiosyncrasy of genius and the pressure he was under in New York. Yes,

Thelma said to herself, my boy is just burdened right now, and soon he'll move back home where he belongs and assume his rightful place in society.

Kenny didn't know who was more delusional, his mother, who believed he would ever want to live under her roof again, or his dad, who had fallen into the habit of handing an apple to anyone who came to the door. An encyclopedia salesman, a lady from the church soliciting donations, and someone who rang their bell by mistake, all commented on the kind gesture and how shiny and juicy the fruit looked. The lady from the church asked for a napkin and starting eating hers in the doorway. Thelma said she could hear crunching noises all the way down the hall. Kenny couldn't help wondering if sometimes his dad didn't do these little things on purpose just to keep his mother guessing.

Between catching up with friends and attending pageant rehearsals and holiday parties with his mother, who kept whipping out his baby pictures and reciting his many scholarly accomplishments in New York, Kenny didn't have much time to himself. One evening, unable to endure another night of Thelma's parading him around like a trophy, he slipped out to the French Quarter with his Big Chief notebook and some freshly sharpened No. 2 pencils. He stopped at dive bars, observing the patrons, their mannerisms and subtle habits, how they talked, what they drank, their quirks. He wanted to internalize them as he did with everyone he mimicked but deeper, harder, more. They would become his family just like the characters from *The Neon Bible*, but this time he vowed to protect them and to do whatever was necessary to ensure their survival. In that moment, he realized who he was: John Kennedy Toole, Writer, and no one could steal that from him. By the time he got back home it was sunrise. He tried to fall asleep but couldn't. He was too excited. He'd nearly filled the entire notebook, and this, he was sure, was just the beginning.

The rest of the semester went quickly. When the day arrived to turn in the final draft of his master's thesis, Kenny moved with uncharacteristic heaviness, his body resisting what his mind had determined was the only way. Years later, he would remember this moment and regret that he'd let himself down. He was almost hoping that his professor would return the document with a large red F and the words "see me immediately" scrawled across the title page. Instead, he got an A, and a note praising the thing along with hearty congratulations on having successfully completed the final step toward his master's degree. So much for higher learning, he thought.

That night, Kenny called Ellen and asked her to go out. She was surprised to hear from him, as he didn't often call. They went out occasionally and talked on the phone, but Kenny was always busy studying or writing. Secretly, he wanted to spend a lot more time with her, but a gentleman always pays for the lady on a date, and he barely had enough money to eat. That evening, Kenny wasn't himself. He was surly and rude, and when he dropped Ellen off at her dorm, she couldn't understand what had happened to him. He didn't mention coming back to her dorm room, and she was hoping he would as her roommate had gone home for the weekend.

Kenny didn't like himself that day. He had cheated the system and won, but it was a hollow victory. On graduation day, he pretended, laughing and joking with his fellow students. Kenny was becoming so good at hiding what was going on inside that sometimes, if he concentrated hard enough, he could even fool himself. He realized he was playing a dangerous game. Unbeknownst to anyone, Kenny had been attending various psychology lectures on campus. He was fascinated by the human mind, its vulnerabilities and strange ways of coping. He told himself he was interested because it would help him write better characters, with more depth and complexity. Sometimes he believed it. Then there were the days like today, when he knew he wasn't searching for answers as a writer, he was trying to understand that part of him that always felt empty. He wanted to figure it out before he didn't care anymore. There was a hole in his soul, he often thought, and he worried that it might swallow him one day, so he did everything he could to protect himself. He nourished his intellect with graduate studies, he wrote, wrote, wrote all the time, he explored the city, met new people, dated because that's what healthy heterosexual boys do, and he was healthy and heterosexual and horny. But he had to be a gentleman and gentlemen don't visit a girl just for sex. No, they wine and dine her. He couldn't afford to court anyone, except his mama, who was insatiable.

Insatiable, that's a good word, he thought. The main character in my New Orleans novel must be insatiable . . . what can I make him crave? What does he want? What is he searching for? He was thinking so fast, his mind whirring like the blades of a blender, that he grabbed his head, pushing on his temples, willing it to stop. Finally, he felt it, one tear, desperate to escape and be joined by the others waiting behind it. Kenny never cried. Men didn't do such things. But he didn't feel like a man in that moment. He felt like a boy, a very, very frightened boy.

He didn't sleep that night. The next morning, he called Ellen and apologized. Then, over coffee on Amsterdam Avenue, he told her the truth, that he thought about her all the time, that he would spend every night with her if he could, but he couldn't afford to pay for everything so that's why he remained aloof sometimes. But it wasn't what his heart felt, he said, taking her hands in his. He seemed to remember a similar scene long ago with Ginny and he blinked the memory away, determined to stay here in the moment with Ellen. After Kenny explained, Ellen hugged him, gently placing his head on her shoulder. Then she paid the check and told him that she was reading *The Second Sex* and if he let her share expenses when they went out, he was contributing to her growth and development as an independent woman, which was very important to her.

With his master's diploma inside one of his Big Chief notebooks and his two suitcases packed, each item neatly folded and in its proper place, John Kennedy Toole said goodbye to Columbia on a hot, muggy morning in the early summer of 1959. As he stood on the corner of 125th Street and Broadway waiting for the bus to the airport, he noticed a sluggishness infecting the city. Everyone around him seemed to be moving slower than usual and looking irritated, their urban costumes clinging to their damp skin, their faces strained, and he realized that perhaps he wasn't the only one coping with the heartlessness of what this city could be for the financially uninitiated. In the cool months, one could fake their love for New York, even convince themselves that the pressure of living there was worth it, but in the sweltering heat of summer, Manhattan exposed its poseurs, those who pretended to enjoy the competitiveness, the unrelenting expectation of perfection, the ambition that shrouded even the most decent people in moral ambiguity when it came to what they would be willing to do to succeed or to survive. He thought about the professor who had praised his thesis. Earlier that day he had telephoned Kenny, asking him about his plans for the future. Kenny said that he was spending the rest of the summer back home and that he had accepted an offer to teach at Southern Louisiana Institute starting in the fall. His professor was aghast that such a promising student would fritter away his talents on a bunch of yahoos in the bayou when he could be pursuing a doctorate. The man's elitist attitude grinded Kenny's craw. Yes, he might eventually become a tenured professor and enjoy prestige and security but he wasn't sure that's what he wanted. Moreover, he couldn't afford it. He tried to explain all this to his professor, but to no avail. Kenny had learned that some professors were so accustomed to lecturing, that even when they weren't at the podium, they still talked that way. Kenny smiled, recalling the philosopher in Washington Square Park on his way to the Gaslight. The poor old guy was warning the world about the coming apocalypse, his voice undulating with conviction. Kenny thought about the differences between the two men, the lonely bum driven by delusion and his English professor, the revered intellectual. Why is it, Kenny wondered, that the hobo preaching under the arches dressed in rags was more interesting? When the bus arrived, Kenny hoisted his bags inside and took a seat. He leaned his cheek against the crack of the open window and closed his eyes, letting his mind rest. By the time the bus finally pulled into LaGuardia, Kenny was anticipating the po'boy he would eat that night and the welcoming embrace of his mother, whom he had begun to miss dearly.

Kenny enjoyed the summer, relishing the familiar. He had forgotten what not having to rush everywhere felt like, and when he left for his teaching post at Southwestern Louisiana Institute in September, he was refreshed and ready. Kenny knew this job wouldn't be without its share of problems. He had been forewarned that many of his students would speak more battered French than English, and that understanding them would require some patience. The day he arrived, he was greeted by a young black student who informed him that he had been given the job of showing their campus to the new professor. He introduced himself as Michael, but told Kenny that everyone called him Gator because he could trap one faster than anybody on the bayou. Kenny laughed. Tulane still didn't allow blacks to enroll. He'd heard Tulane referred to as the Harvard of the South, but that kind of ignorance made such a comparison ridiculous. The Institute was the first college in Louisiana to accept black students after the 1954 *Brown v. Board of Education* decision that rendered segregation on campuses unconstitutional. As Kenny toured the campus, it reminded him more of a Southern plantation with its lush, verdant gardens and sprawling shade trees than a school. Gator pointed out the history of certain buildings, pausing occasionally so that the new professor could ask questions. Kenny couldn't help but smile at his earnestness. Though his clothes were worn-looking and his pants beginning to fray at the cuff, they were clean and pressed. Kenny took an immediate liking to this kid. He didn't carry the pall of unresolved resentment nor did he expect anything from the world that he wasn't willing to work hard for. Kenny began to feel better about his decision to teach here. Though he hadn't admitted it to anyone, the telephone conversation with his professor had unnerved him. He wondered, What if he was right, that he was making a mistake?

"Come on, I'll show you where your classroom is," Gator said.

Kenny was tired from the walk through the campus and suggested they sit down by what looked like a storage facility up ahead.

"Those aren't storage buildings," Gator said. "That's the English department."

Kenny thought the dilapidated army surplus buildings made of corrugated steel resembled Quonset huts. No longer a charming plantation, this part of campus resembled an abandoned barracks.

"It ain't that bad, Professor Toole," Gator said.

Gator escorted Kenny to his classroom. The door was rusted and difficult to open, the desks were in need of repair, and the chalkboard had a crack through the middle. The floorboards were flimsy and each time Kenny took a step, he could feel them shifting beneath his feet. Everything about this place screamed "get out while you still can," but Kenny couldn't hear it. Maybe it was Gator's optimistic spirit or the stark contrast between this spot and the rest of the university that gave Kenny pause. He thought of diamonds and how they start out rough, unrecognizable until someone cuts them and transforms them into jewels. Perhaps the teachers here were the cutters and students like Gator the diamonds. Kenny had experienced a crown jewel of universities and it left him feeling no more fulfilled than before he'd arrived. This English department was a diamond waiting to be polished.

It didn't take Kenny long to settle in. He found a modest furnished apartment in an old converted carriage house. His landlady was no Thelma Toole. The kitchen was dingy and gray, there were grease stains on the ceiling, and the bathroom looked as if it hadn't been cleaned in months. On move-in day, he spent all afternoon scrubbing the apartment, grateful for a place to call his own. Some of the neighbors could hear him humming through the open window. As he was unpacking his toiletries, Kenny observed a large spider crawling across the sink. He wrestled with what to do. He could leave it alone to spin its web and be a bug catcher or he could use the newspaper that was sitting by the front table to swat it. He remembered the night that he trapped fireflies in jars.

Kenny scooped the creature onto a tissue and moved it to the corner. "You'll be okay there, buddy."

Kenny enjoyed getting to know the other faculty members. They were a cast of personalities not unlike the regulars at Washington Square Park. Their eccentricities and quirks humanized them to students, creating an inclusive learning environment. None was more memorable than the strange and fascinating professor with whom he shared an office. Kenny sometimes wondered if he tumbled out of a time machine and had simply wandered into the English department. Kenny tried to describe him in one of his Big Chief notebooks, but every time he thought he had finally captured him, he'd cross out what he'd written and start again. He'd never had this problem before. When Kenny sat down to write, the words flowed freely. His biggest challenge was turning it off. When he allowed the author inside him to be free it was like flying, and he never, ever wanted to come down. Writing about this colleague was making him feel like he did that day in English class with Ginny, when the teacher asked him about Chaucer, and he knew the answer but just couldn't get it out. John Kennedy Toole would conquer writer's block only one more time in his life, and like this moment, it would put in motion a sequence of events that many would look back on in disbelief.

The days passed quickly and Kenny made friends with his colleagues and students. He felt honored and valued. He looked forward to each morning and seeing his students'

faces, always eager to listen, hungry to learn. The girls would
gossip about his elegant attire, how he always wore a jacket
and tie, and walked briskly with his shoulders back, confident
and focused, and on cool days how he'd casually fling a scarf
around his neck. Gator was one of his best students. He loved
literature and wanted to teach at the new high school they
were building down by the oil refineries. He would be the first
college graduate in his family. Kenny saw in Gator an unlikely
kid brother. He was ravenous for knowledge and could distill
literary intentions easily. One evening he and Gator had a
long conversation about love and revolution and the power of
writers to capture their essence. They spoke of Moloch and
Rockland and angel-headed hipsters. They talked of drunken
boats and the melancholy moonlight "sweet and lone." Kenny
taught Gator how to appreciate a writer's skill. Gator was
smart. Kenny saw it and took pride in him. He'd often wanted
a sibling and couldn't understand why his parents only had
one child. When he'd ask his mother, she'd tell him that
when he was born, he was so perfect that she couldn't imagine
being able to love another child as she loved him, and that it
wouldn't be fair. Hearing that never made him feel special, just
burdened. He longed for a brother or sister to assume some of
that love and the expectations that went along with it, not to
mention having someone to help him with the responsibility
of his parents as they aged. Kenny thought parents who chose
to have only one child were selfish.

At Southern Louisiana Institute, Kenny learned to be
content with himself. Despite having put on a few pounds

thanks to Cajun cooking, Kenny never felt lighter. Perhaps all those people who were fat and happy were onto something. He wasn't fat yet but he was definitely bordering on rotund. The added weight, rather than making him self-conscious, seemed to embolden his humor. When he mimicked someone now, he took it much further. He felt alive and free in this unlikely place of discovery. One of his favorite drinking buddies was Joel. The son of the university president, Joel was the same age as Kenny. He was working for the school newspaper. They were both raised to be polite, elegant, and refined. Sometimes after a few beers and a long week of being perfect gentlemen, they'd talk about the hypocrisy of many of the social conventions they were taught to honor. Kenny suspected Joel might be gay and it endeared him to Kenny even more. Kenny knew what it was like to struggle with something you couldn't control and to have a parent whom you were terrified of disappointing.

As the semester neared its end, Kenny received a phone call from New York. His professor, the same one that had attempted to dissuade his teaching at the Institute, said that he'd secured him an assistant professorship at Hunter College starting in the fall.

"You'll be able to earn enough to complete your doctorate," the professor said. "You'd be foolish to refuse this opportunity."

Kenny couldn't conjure an argument. He wasn't sure it was what he wanted. All he could hear was his mother's voice, telling him how proud she was, and that this was the moment she'd been waiting for. Without enthusiasm, Kenny accepted the offer. That summer, he and Joel spent time together going out with friends and experiencing New Orleans as only young men can.

It was 1960. Ted Williams hit his five-hundredth home run, the birth control pill was introduced in America, and an eighteen-year-old unknown named Aretha Franklin had her first recording session. As summer surrendered its embrace, Kenny readied himself for New York. While he was packing, he thought about the past year and the friends he'd made in the bayou, the joy he'd found there. Whatever lay ahead, he wasn't the same person who had ridden that sweltering, hot bus from 125th Street to LaGuardia Airport a year earlier.

He'd always wonder if he had left behind a life that might have held more promise than he'd realized. On lonely nights, when he had nothing but his thoughts and the hands on his clock reminding him that he'd have to be up in two hours, yet sleep still hadn't come, he'd speculate about the bayou and if he'd stayed, would he have finished his novel, maybe found a girl there, married her, and had kids? Kenny didn't like pondering the what-ifs, but SLI had left its imprint: the lovable, unkempt professor who quoted Boethius and wore different color socks, his long talks with Gator, the warmth and camaraderie. He had been content and hadn't known it. He missed the place.

———

Kenny was frantic. He was taking five graduate courses at Columbia, planning his doctoral thesis, and teaching a full load of classes at Hunter. Columbia and Hunter were at opposite sides of the city. The train was pulling up. He'd never make it. He quickened his pace. His head was pounding. He was out of breath. He was running now. Just as the doors began to close, he wedged his body between them and pushed his way inside. The train was packed. He leaned against the railing. Did he finish grading all those papers and what about his notes for the lecture tomorrow, did he have them or were they in his desk at the apartment? The apartment, the rent check, did he mail the rent check, no it was still on the kitchen table. Mail, damn it, he also forgot to mail his parents a check.

Thelma would be asking him because she always asked, and asked and asked, and he couldn't lie, she knew when he was lying, but she didn't care if he lied to himself, no, that was fine as long as he was doing what she wanted, what everyone wanted, and his uncle Arthur, he hadn't written him a letter yet, think, think, yes, tomorrow he'd get up early tomorrow and write his uncle a letter about Hunter and his students. *Craw, craw, craw,* that's what some of the girls sounded like, always raising their hands, wanting to participate, but what difference did it make because most of them will give up their careers to raise babies and what's the point of going through midterms and tests and papers if all you're going to do is give it up anyway and raise babies, and one of them was lying to him about why she was late with her paper, he had seen her out on a date the night she claimed she had been at a funeral and, Faulkner, that's right, the paper was on Faulkner, and she said the way he dressed reminded her of Faulkner, and that was lovely, Kenny thought, and was he there yet, did he miss his stop?

He needed a break from the city. He'd lost weight. His complexion was gray and his eyes, normally bright and alive, had dimmed. He didn't tell anyone about the trip. His mother couldn't understand why he didn't want to come home for Thanksgiving. He said he had to study. She didn't push him. She knew her son and when he was determined, it was best to leave things be. Kenny had heard some of his colleagues talking about what a wonderful place Nantucket was to visit. A week later, on the day before Thanksgiving, he slipped away with one small overnight bag and his toiletries.

Kenny had to take a train to Boston and then a ferry to reach the island. As the ferry pulled into port, he felt all the tension from the past few months recede and everything before him appeared crisp and bright. He was immediately struck by Nantucket's beauty. A restful island off the coast, where the men wore faded, red trousers, and all the houses were painted white, the only divergence was the color of the shutters. Apparently, households could select the paint in any color, as long as it was black or dark green. He wondered how often someone, returning late from a restaurant or dinner party, tried to let themselves into a house that was not theirs.

Kenny found a tiny inn by the beach. He was surprised how affordable the room was. The proprietor, a gaunt woman in her late sixties, was friendly but reserved in that New England way. Kenny could tell she was a smoker. When she spoke, her voice was raspy and there were lines around her mouth from years of lips pursed around a cigarette. She asked Kenny why he was there over a holiday, didn't he have any family? He explained that he was a writer living in New York, and was seeking a break from everything, especially family. She must have found Kenny's honesty disarming because for a brief moment, she smiled warmly as if to say, I could tell you some stories about that, young man. She showed him his room. It contained a bed, a desk with a reading light, a chair, and a utilitarian commode. The view was spectacular. All Kenny could see out the window was ocean.

"It's nothing fancy, but it's warm and nobody will bother you here," she said.

"It's perfect."

After unpacking his toothbrush and comb, and hanging up the few items of clothing he'd brought, he donned his hat, scarf, and gloves and went for a long walk on the beach. It was cold and the wind was fierce. A few locals exchanged befuddled glances as they watched him pass, wondering who the stranger was going for a beach stroll as if it were the dog days of summer. Kenny coveted the tempered violence of the atmosphere, how the wind was just loud enough to compete with the roar of the surf, how the sand circled and blew. It was an overcast day and it had just begun to drizzle. Kenny wasn't sure how long he walked, but by the time he again saw the inn in the distance, the sun had nearly set. He stopped, closed his eyes, threw back his head, and let the rain and the sea and the salt and the wind assail his senses, awaken his imagination. He breathed it all in. In that moment, standing on that blustery wet day on a beach in Nantucket, he made himself a promise.

SIX

Reporter Bill Greeley stood with the wind on his back, staring at the ocean, questioning his decision. He had made it hastily. Maybe he should have considered his options more carefully. He had felt stifled in Minneapolis, as if his purpose lay elsewhere. He was single, only thirty-five years old, and ready for adventure. The East Coast was expensive and the freelance competition fierce. There was always someone else willing to fight for a good story. The ideal of journalistic integrity was absent from a lot of writers. He closed his eyes and let the sounds and smells of the beach calm him. The temperature continued to drop and he hugged his jacket, wishing he had brought at least one sweater along on this assignment. It was unusually cold for June even for Nantucket. The reporter's mind drifted. While

Horace Greeley had said "Go West Young Man," his distant relative saw the future in the opposite direction. A childhood and education in Minnesota lead Bill Greeley to a job on the *Minneapolis Star-Tribune*. A three-part, much-admired article on the town Sinclair Lewis immortalized brought an opportunity to freelance in New York, a roving commission to cover and report on the arts, which for this reporter meant music and movies.

And so it was not surprising to find Bill Greeley in New England at one of the most popular and anticipated American film festivals, looking for a story he could sell. Only he had no idea what the story would be. He was on his own dime at the Nantucket Film Festival, having finagled a press pass from the entertainment editor at the *New York Post*. The deal was simple. If the *Post* liked the story, they'd pay him and pick up his expenses. If not, he might find a restful few days in the fresh air.

The year is 2003. The average price of a new home is a quarter of a million dollars. Arnold Schwarzenegger is elected governor of California, Saddam Hussein is captured by U.S. forces, and Apple launches iTunes.

The damp, chilly weather was beginning to seep into his bones but Greeley loved the ocean, her grace and power, the way her waves kept returning to the shore, curling into the sand like thick wild tresses she was letting down as she greeted him. He started walking briskly along the beach back to the cozy seaside inn where he was staying. He smiled for maybe the first time since he'd moved out East. He wondered if other writers and dreamers had discovered their courage on this very beach and if they'd accomplished those dreams. He didn't know that four decades earlier, one of them, twenty-three-year old Kenny Toole, had left his footprints there.

When Greeley returned to his room, there was a package waiting for him. It included a press kit for the film festival and a list of screenings and events. He decided to review the contents over a drink in the hotel bar. As he made his way down to the lobby, he stopped to look at a collage of photos on the wall depicting the inn over the years. The proprietor noticed him admiring the photos and asked if there was anything about the inn he'd like to know. Greeley was struck by the woman's natural beauty. She was older than he, in her forties he guessed, but one of those women who looked younger than her years, her skin freshened by ocean air. She was wearing no makeup except for a bit of lip gloss and her cheeks were rosy, as if she'd just been outside. She explained that the inn was built in the early 1800s and was originally the private home of a whaling captain and his family. Her grandparents bought it in 1932 and turned it into an inn.

"My fondest memories are here," she said. "There was a time I thought about selling it but something kept me from going through with it. This place is just so full of history." Greeley invited her to join him for a drink. For the next hour, she amused him with stories about the inn and some of the famous guests that had stayed there. She talked about her grandmother and how after her grandfather passed, she stayed on and ran the inn.

"Nana was a real trouper. She preferred the island during the off-season and kept the inn open all winter. She always said that the travelers who visited in the coldest months were the most interesting folks she got."

Then she told Greeley about one guest in particular who stayed over Thanksgiving weekend 1960 that her grandmother remembered. "Nana said she'd never forget that Thanksgiving because it was the day that Wilt Chamberlain got fifty-five rebounds in a game against the Boston Celtics."

Greeley was captivated.

"Nana didn't mention this guest's name but there was something about him that never left her, he was just this sweet kid in his early twenties, yet in his eyes she could see a thousand untold stories. And he spoke with a Southern accent that Nana said made her want to hear all those stories."

"Do you have any idea who it might have been?" Greeley asked.

"No, but Nana said what struck her the most, the thing that she couldn't understand, was how such a gifted boy with so much life ahead of him seemed so burdened. He told her he hated his job teaching at some big university in New York, that all he wanted was to be a writer, and that he'd made a secret promise to himself. The way he said it made her sad."

"Did he tell her what that promise was?" Greeley asked.

"No, and she always wondered what happened to him, if he kept that promise. You're actually staying in the same room that he did."

Greeley began ticking off the names of famous Southern writers from that era: Reynolds Price, Peter Taylor, they would have been in their early twenties back then, Greeley thought, or maybe William Styron, when was he born? Flannery O'Connor! No, that was a woman. Greeley kept running through the possibilities, trying to figure out the identity of the stranger. Greeley must have seemed miles away to the gracious proprietor, who politely mentioned that it was getting late and that she had to be up early. Greeley thanked her for a lovely evening. When he got back to his room, he sat at the desk and began going through the press kit for the film festival. He opened the drawer, looking for a pen or pencil, when he noticed something. Someone had carved their initials. It read, I.R., NOVEMBER, 1960. Greeley could think of no famous writer with those initials.

He turned back to the task at hand: finding a story to cover at the film festival. Everything listed was standard fare, nothing that every other writer wouldn't be covering, and probably scoring more interviews because they had been attending the festival since its inception. Then he saw that Steven Soderbergh was doing a staged reading of *A Confederacy of Dunces* at Nantucket High School. He had tried to read that book in college but couldn't get past the first twenty pages. It seemed to go on and on, like *War and Peace*. Admittedly he wasn't a connoisseur of literary fiction, finding it pretentious. Long-winded tomes didn't interest him. Still, this event could have potential. He'd heard about previous attempts to turn the book into a film and how some people believed there was a curse on the project. He vaguely recalled an article from a few years back about how many of the actors who'd been considered for the lead role had died before they could do the film.

As Greeley went to bed that night, he thought about the memorable guest at the inn and wondered if the initials he found in the desk could have been his. The next morning, he asked the proprietor if there was a way to learn who had stayed there that long-ago Thanksgiving.

"Nana kept guest logs. If you don't mind a little dust, I have them in the storage room."

Within an hour, they found the log for 1960. Greeley felt like a kid on a scavenger hunt. They turned to November 24. It read: "John Kennedy Toole, New York, New York."

"I've seen that name somewhere," the proprietor said. She walked over to the library located off the lobby, searching the shelves. She pulled out a copy of *A Confederacy of Dunces*.

"This has been part of our collection for years. Books left by visitors."

She opened it. Inside was an inscription from 1981, "To the next guest at this lovely inn, I hope you get as much joy from this wonderful book as I did."

Greeley thanked her, walked out to his rental car, and drove to the high school. As he arrived, it hit him. "I.R., Ignatius Reilly!" The future author of *A Confederacy of Dunces* had carved his protagonist's initials into the desk. Greeley was envisioning his article when the house lights dimmed and the actors took the stage. The program listed Will Ferrell as Ignatius. Greeley had never been a fan of Will Ferrell, thinking his acting style too broad. Though he'd enjoyed his work on *Saturday Night Live*, Ferrell simply wasn't someone Greeley thought about. Until now. Ferrell's only prop was Ignatius's signature green hunting cap. Greeley watched in disbelief as the tall, curly-haired actor with long, slender hands and an angular face transformed into a fat, bloated blowhard waving his paws in indignation at the world. Ferrell's entrance was nothing less than inspired. He emerged from the back of the theater shouting insults at the other actors as the narrator introduced them. For a moment, Greeley was reminded of his childhood idol Andy Kaufman, whose infamous alter ego, Tony Clifton, with the same mop of hair and curmudgeonly disposition, would hurl invectives like grenades. Ferrell's Ignatius convinced Greeley that maybe he hadn't given the book a chance. Yes, he thought, tonight I have a date with John Kennedy Toole. He decided that his article would bring to life the tale of a film project. He was hoping to talk with Will Ferrell, but missed him. He chatted with Paul Rudd, Anne Meara, Mos Def, and even got a quote from Soderbergh.

What struck Greeley most was everyone's reverence for Toole. There was an unspoken sadness that the author wasn't there to share in the excitement. Greeley didn't believe in anything he couldn't see or touch. He was raised by a crusty old pragmatist, his father, a veteran newspaper man, and his mother, a no-nonsense school teacher. He was a throwback to another era, an old-fashioned journalist who felt responsible for the truth and preferred a legal pad for taking notes instead of a laptop. To Greeley, half the people who called themselves reporters nowadays were as full of shit as a Minnesota Christmas turkey. Yes, Greeley was a cynic, but he couldn't help but think that Toole's spirit might have been present at that reading, that everything that had happened in the past twenty-four hours smacked of more than coincidence. "Shake it off, Greeley," he told himself.

That night, Greeley began reading the inn's copy of the novel. He started as soon as he returned to his room and at 3:00 A.M., he was still awake, unable to stop. Though he wouldn't admit this to anyone, he still found himself skipping past the long parts. He felt guilty, but every time Ignatius erupted into one of his rambling soliloquies against the establishment, the reporter who had been trained that less was more and who'd refused to read Updike in college on principle simply couldn't understand why the publisher never edited the damn thing. In fact, as he started the research for his article, there was a lot he didn't understand. Yes, it was heartbreaking that Toole didn't live to see his masterpiece published, but would this book have had the same appeal if the author had gone on a multicity tour, humming happily to himself at his first book signing, convivial and effusive, eager to connect with the fans who had lined up for hours awaiting his arrival? Would a publisher even consider a tour in the first place? Did all the drama and mystery behind this book contribute more to its success than was politic to admit? Tragedy has legs, thought Greeley. What if Ignatius Reilly stormed America in the mid-sixties when Toole was still here and the world wasn't ready for him? What if this book had been a flop, an obscure title destined for the remainder tables? How do we know it would have been the phenomenon it became if events had unfolded differently?

Greeley double-checked the date of original publication against the author's obituary. It wasn't published until eleven years after Toole died. What was going on? Was there an agent? Was the manuscript sent to New York publishers? Did they all turn it down? And if they had published it eleven years earlier, would it have found an audience? Greeley wondered if the decade delay may have been the making of the novel's popularity.

When he returned to New York, Greeley met with a favorite professor from college, Dr. Bell, who had recently joined the faculty at the NYU School of Journalism. An award-winning reporter who had a few close calls chasing stories in war-torn Third World countries, he shifted to academics when his daughter was born. She'd recently married and moved to New Jersey, so when the serendipitous offer came from NYU, he and his wife moved to Manhattan to be nearer to their only child. Rotund and affable, the man was always available. Greeley couldn't remember him ever coming to class in a bad mood. Though he didn't speak much about his years in the field, Greeley suspected that something happened out there that left him grateful just to be alive. He never worried about the little things and taught his students that above all else, they must, as journalists, always be guided by truth and integrity. It was the last one, he'd often say, that many of his colleagues struggled with, and for him, it was never about ethics, which was too philosophical a discussion, it was about how you treated people. Greeley was eager to discuss with him how best to approach his article. Though the professor's journalistic expertise would be helpful, it was his hobby that Greeley wanted to tap into. Professor Bell was a movie buff. He also had contacts in Hollywood that he'd cultivated over the years. Professor Bell suggested they meet for a drink at the Knickerbocker on University Place.

A bustling restaurant near NYU's Washington Square campus, the Knickerbocker was reminiscent of a 1920s Paris bistro with an American jazz influence. Its regulars well represented Greenwich Village. When Greeley arrived, he saw his mentor sitting at the bar reading the *New York Times*. The two men greeted each other and ordered lunch along with a sturdy Côte du Rhône. It wasn't until Greeley looked at his watch that he realized nearly two hours had passed. As the bartender cleared their plates and brought out two glasses of Sauternes on the house, Greeley addressed the reason he wanted to meet.

Professor Bell listened as Greeley recounted what he'd learned, the author's tragic death eleven years before the book was published, the long list of directors and producers who'd attempted a film version, and how no one could get the damn thing out of development hell, all the actors that kept dropping dead after their names came up to play the lead, a murder-suicide, a hurricane, and God knows what else, Greeley said, that almost made him think there might be a curse.

The professor became curious. He'd read *A Confederacy of Dunces* years before, and recalled the *New York Times* had not reviewed the book in hardcover. Christopher Lehmann-Haupt, who missed his opportunity when it first came out, reviewed it when it was released in paperback a year later, justifying his omission by suggesting the novel was anti-Semitic, a view that Bell considered an unfortunate excuse.

"I read it in 1981, and the author had been dead over a decade by then. Why did it take so long to get published?" asked Bell.

"Well, for one thing, it sat in an editor's office at Simon & Schuster for almost three years."

"Wasn't there another novel from Simon & Schuster that was similar to Toole's, but not nearly as good?"

"Someone mentioned that to me in Nantucket, I'll have to look," Greeley said.

"The title was awful, almost put me off on reading the damn thing," Professor Bell said. "Came out years before *A Confederacy of Dunces*. I was still in grad school. Only reason I remember is because I was doing book reviews at the time for the university paper and someone had given me a copy. I wish I could recall the name of it. When was Toole's manuscript with Simon & Schuster?"

Greeley recognized that look right away. Greeley and Bell understood each other. They loved putting together the pieces of something scattered long ago that begged to be assembled, the remnants of something that should have been told, a narrative waiting to be woven. Yes, Greeley had a good reputation and so did his mentor, but they were driven by something larger, the satisfaction of seeing a story where no one else did. Greeley suspected he was onto something when he found those initials carved in that desk in Nantucket. Now he was certain. This story was just stirring to life.

Greeley was so lost in thought that Professor Bell had to repeat the question.

"Sorry, Professor. Based on what I could find out so far, Toole first sent his manuscript to Simon & Schuster around 1964."

"Is the editor still alive?"

"Yes, his name is Robert Gottlieb."

"I've met him," Bell said. "At Lincoln Center, some fundraiser for the ballet. It was a while ago. We chatted about Balanchine. I liked him. Very impressive man."

"Do you think it was possible he was the editor of that similar book you mentioned?"

"It's worth finding out. If so, it gives you another avenue for your story."

Greeley's mind was whirling. The more he sat there, the more he felt a story moving within him. "Do you know anything about Barney Rosset and Grove Press?"

"He was a big deal back in the day. He was the first publisher to take on censorship in America and win. I interviewed him once. Struck me as a very different fellow than the S&S editor."

"How so?"

"Both are men of letters, intelligent, committed to good writers, but Rosset is another animal entirely. He's all intuition and repressed sexuality, the smartest sixteen-year-old you'd ever want to meet. Didn't Grove Press publish *A Confederacy of Dunces*?"

"Louisiana State University published it first, but they only planned on printing a few hundred copies until Grove got a hold of the paperback rights. A young editor there fought for the book, got everyone who was anyone to review it."

"It did seem like that book appeared out of nowhere," Professor Bell observed. "All of a sudden, you couldn't turn around without seeing someone reading it."

"What did you think?"

"There are certain books that when you recall reading them, you remember exactly what was happening at the time. I was in Poland covering the Solidarity movement when I read *Dunces*. The situation there was dangerous for journalists, especially from the U.S. I was traveling with a group. Everyone was on edge. One night I was reading to try to fall asleep and started laughing. My colleagues insisted on knowing what was so funny, so I started reading out loud. It was the first time since we arrived that we felt relaxed, just a bunch of ink-stained wretches laughing their asses off at something truly hilarious. Ignatius's mishaps reminded us of the absurdity of it all. The next day, soldiers seized control of the country and martial law went into effect."

Greeley wondered how many other stories were out there about this book and if Toole was aware that his work would leave an imprint like a tattoo on its readers.

"You may need to go back to the beginning," Professor Bell said. "Why that book took so long to get published. Who was responsible or not. And why a small university press, when Simon & Schuster had been interested? Why didn't another

New York publisher grab it? You may find things that will surprise you."

As Greeley listened to Bell, he thought more about John Kennedy Toole. They would have been about the same age had Toole survived. Though Greeley didn't know Professor Bell as a younger man, he imagined he was a person you'd want as a friend, someone who was not only loyal but intuitive. Greeley remembered this one classmate. He wore his shirts starched, his jeans with a crease, and he had a pair of white Nike high-tops that always looked like new. One morning, he came to class with his shoelaces missing. It was odd but no one thought much of it, except the professor. Years later at an alumni event, Greeley spoke with the classmate. He told Greeley he was missing shoe-laces that day because he'd tried to hang himself but realized rope would probably work better. He never got to the hardware store because Professor Bell asked him to stay after class and kept him there until he'd admitted he was struggling and needed help. Were there any warning signs on the day of John Kennedy Toole's death? Would someone have noticed a missing shoelace? Would it have mattered? Research for Greeley meant not only unearthing facts, but finding the human element behind them. It wouldn't be easy chasing down leads decades old. He would follow this story wherever it took him.

"Walk me through again what you've got on the movie," Professor Bell said.

Greeley took out his notes and began enumerating the high points, starting with Scott Kramer, the young production assistant at Fox who bought the film rights for ten thousand dollars back in 1980, how he convinced Johnny Carson to greenlight the project and John Belushi to play the lead. "But two nights before Belushi is scheduled to meet with Kramer, he dies of an overdose. Then, the head of the Louisiana State Film Commission, another key player, is killed by her husband in a murder-suicide."

Professor Bell leaned back and listened.

"Carson bails after that and then some Texas oil tycoon and his girlfriend buy the rights for a quarter of a million. She bumps into John Candy in the waiting room at a weight-loss clinic and while they're sitting there, gets him interested in playing Ignatius. It doesn't work out. Then Candy dies, too."

Professor Bell ordered another round.

"The Texans run out of money. They try to get investors but can't find any takers, except maybe Toole's mother, had she been asked but she wasn't, and boy was she angry."

"Can't blame her," Professor Bell said.

"She's another story. By the way, did I mention the tycoon and his girlfriend were working out of some funeral home in New Orleans?"

This is the stuff of a Beckett play, Greeley thought. It was as if John Kennedy were orchestrating all of it from the grave. Taking a sip of wine, he envisioned a mischievous-eyed Toole, now a gamer with a remote control in his hands, sitting in front of a giant movie screen connected to some weird cosmic PlayStation, laughing as he manipulated his avatars. If Greeley knew Toole, and he felt as if he was getting to know him better every day, this was just the beginning.

"Next, Orion Pictures gets involved, convinces Harold Ramis to direct, but they want a svelte, buff Ignatius. Ramis is appalled."

Professor Bell shook his head. "It wouldn't be the first time a brilliant book almost got mangled beyond recognition. I once met Mickey Rooney in Chicago. We started to chat and he told me that he never understood being cast as Chinese, but he took the job because he adored Audrey Hepburn and he needed the money."

"You're talking about *Breakfast at Tiffany's*."

"And some books had it even worse when Hollywood got their fingers on them. Lucky Jim was one unlucky bastard."

Greeley smiled. He missed this man.

"What about *Love Story*! Heavens to Christ, it's a good thing I saw that nonsense on an empty stomach. If they were making the Melville novel now, I could only imagine the talk around the production table. 'Does anyone remember, was Moby-Dick the sailor or the whale?'"

Between the good French wine and spirited conversation, both men lost track of time, until the early happy hour crowd started arriving.

"How much time has gone by at this point?" asked the professor.

"Almost a decade. Fast forward to 1992. Ramis is out. The Texan is back in. He hires a real producer. She goes to Cannes, pitches the project to New Line, and gets this confused look. They tell her that Scott Kramer and Steven Soderbergh already pitched them. And miraculously enough, everyone was willing to play nice together in the sandbox. Enter network television veteran Brandon Tartikoff wanting to join in. He suggests Chris Farley for the lead. That doesn't work out, and then both of them die."

"If Thomas Hardy were alive, he'd be taking notes."

Greeley realized that he didn't know much about any of these people.

"I can see why Soderbergh suspects a curse," Bell said. "What's happened since?"

"Soderbergh wants to move on, but Kramer won't let go. He finds a director, gets Miramax to put up one and a half million. That brings us to the reading at the Nantucket Film Festival."

"It's 2003. Surely this thing will be made," Professor Bell opined. "Two more years and it will have been a quarter century since Kramer first optioned the rights."

"The book was a huge success when it was finally published, and now it's considered a classic. Maybe the universe has a similar timetable for the movie."

"Toole, like many brilliant creatives, may have tapped into something earlier than the rest of us, but I have to wonder, if he had lived, would the film have happened any faster?"

Greeley hadn't thought about that. He considered all the magnificent books that were turned into films long after the authors had died: *Little Women*, *Treasure Island*, *A Christmas Carol*, the list was endless. What about those that were never made? The first one that came to mind was *The Catcher in the Rye*. Maybe that's the category where *A Confederacy of Dunces* should reside. Maybe it really wasn't meant to be made into a movie.

As the two men said their goodbyes, promising to meet again soon, Greeley decided to postpone the article for the *New York Post*. He needed to immerse himself in the research. Something was tugging at him. It felt as if John Kennedy Toole himself was reaching out, wanting him to tell the true story.

"Okay, Kenny, where do you want me to look first?"

SEVEN

———◦◦◦———

I t had been six months since Kenny returned to New Orleans from his duty at Fort Buchanan. He was now teaching at Dominican College, an all-girls school near Tulane, and helping to support the family. The heady idealism that he'd felt on the flight from Puerto Rico had been replaced by quiet, nagging disappointment. It seemed that every time he achieved some independence, he ended up where he began, living in an apartment with two people who loved him dearly and made him feel trapped.

Thelma had changed during the two years he served in the army. It saddened Kenny that his mother treated his father as if he were an aging pet that needed to be put out of its misery.

Kenny assumed that Thelma always made herself scarce when he had visitors over in order to give her son and his friends their privacy. The truth was that Thelma simply couldn't bear how they looked at her, a combination of pity and disdain. She wanted her only child to be proud of both his parents and it hurt that she couldn't give that to him.

It wasn't only things at home that were bothering Kenny. The world seemed strange and unfamiliar since President Kennedy was killed. Though Kenny didn't consider himself political, there was something ennobling about John F. Kennedy. When he listened to Kennedy speak, it awakened his patriotism. It was the first time a politician had given Kenny faith in his own future. When he learned of the assassination, it was as if he had lost a close friend. On campus that week, the mood was somber and his students who were usually flirtatious were withdrawn, their demeanor clouded with grief. Kenny had believed that one day he would meet the president and have a long conversation with him about philosophy and literature. When he knew he'd never have that intimate talk with Jack, he despaired, not only over a great man's passing, but a hope dashed.

Kenny recalled his trip to Nantucket three years earlier, just weeks after Kennedy had been elected. There was so much excitement on campus that month, the optimism was palpable even among the cynics in the English department. It was as if a collective exhalation had spread across the country. Kenny had thought about the inauguration during the ferry ride from Boston.

Later, as the situation in Vietnam escalated, and the new president's policy seemed to dictate more bloodshed, Kenny witnessed his classmates at Columbia protesting the war. Kenny could feel the anger of those who pleaded the case for peace. He wondered if that unusual girl Joanie, whom he'd met at the Gaslight, was standing on a stage singing her outrage, her voice like a bell ringing through the cold, indifferent night, as news crews hovered, capturing the country's unrest. Kenny could almost feel the sea spray from that ferry ride as he contemplated his commitment to freedom, weighing it against his respect for human life. He recalled standing outside on the deck, his eyes stinging from the wind and salt, wondering if he was wrong not to have protested along with them. He didn't believe in war, either. He didn't want young American soldiers killed in jungles with names no one could even pronounce.

When he got back to Columbia after that weekend, something inside him had changed. Maybe it was the kind proprietress who had been interested when he told her about his dream of becoming a novelist. Her silent listening had clarified his purpose. Or maybe it was the long walk on the beach and making that promise. Whatever it was, it stayed with him the rest of the academic year, punctuating his ambiguity about New York. When he received his draft papers, he was secretly relieved. The chances of combat were remote. The army just needed him to teach, and if he was going somewhere, why not sunny Puerto Rico? Yes, it had been a good two years. His life in New York, running between Columbia and Hunter, had become exhausting. The draft rescued him. And it allowed him to father Ignatius. Now he was back in New Orleans, and Ignatius was burning inside him, begging for release.

The holidays had been forced. It wasn't the big things that got to Kenny; it was the small, stultifying exchanges between his parents, the way Thelma shook her head when the old man stained the toilet, frantically scrubbing it clean before anyone else saw the evidence of what she had to live with. The way J.D. would reach for Thelma's hand and she'd pull away. The moments Thelma would glare at her husband, wishing he'd snap out of whatever had stolen him from her, and he'd leave the room, the pads of his tired, worn-out slippers punctuating the silence.

Kenny felt sorry for them both. Why didn't his dad fight back? He remembered his dad always pushing him to try harder, like when he was struggling with long division and J.D. would make him practice until he could do it backward and forward. Why couldn't his dad find that part of himself now, instead of just giving in?

It was 1964. A cultural wave was rolling across the United States: Italian films, British music, and the coming tsunami of the sexual revolution. The Beatles had captivated America on *The Ed Sullivan Show*. Andy Warhol had painted his *Triple Elvis* and would soon pair it with *Four Marlons*. No one was mistaking Warhol for Willem de Kooning, Elvis for Cole Porter, or Brando for Cary Grant. The nation was still reeling from the assassination of President Kennedy. Martin Luther King Jr. had won the Nobel Peace Prize. The average yearly income was six thousand dollars.

The start of spring semester was a welcome distraction for Kenny from the tension at home. His thoughts drifted to his students at Dominican. He needed their adoration, the way in which they responded to him. They fought to get into his classes. They enjoyed how he challenged them to question the world. They laughed at his humor and delighted in his impromptu performances. Kenny felt like a king in class. It was the one place, other than at his typewriter, where he was in control. He loved the brisk stroll to campus each morning, the dried leaves crunching under his feet; it was the journey home in the afternoons that sapped his spirit. Every step closer to the front door seemed heavier than the one before it. He wanted to find Dad reading the newspaper or doing the crossword puzzle when he walked in, perhaps complaining about a little arthritis in his left knee or that he might be getting cataracts: the normal, predictable meanderings of an elderly parent, not this spectacle of a father drifting in and out of reality, afraid of the woman at the dining room table going through his mail, cursing under her breath, yearning for someone to rescue her and tell her everything she longed to hear, but instead she waited for her son to come home from school.

Kenny was so lost in his own head that he almost didn't see his father coming down the hall.

"Dad, your fly?"

J.D. looked down and stared at his trousers. His son reached over and zipped him up. Then Kenny retreated to his room, put on the pair of fresh pajamas that his mom had carefully laid out on his bed, went to his desk, and continued reading where he had left off the night before. Only fifteen more pages and his manuscript would be ready to send to the first publisher. Kenny had done considerable research on how to submit a manuscript. He could try finding an agent but suspected that unless you knew someone, getting their attention might be challenging. He was also put off by this notion of a query letter. He'd asked one of his professors at Columbia about literary agents, and learned that you had to send a query first that outlined the premise of the book and why anyone should want to read it.

"You mean like a book report?" Kenny asked.

His professor laughed. He'd never heard it put that way before. By the time they got off the phone, Kenny decided it was better to submit the manuscript directly to editors. Besides, he had no idea how to describe what this book was about nor who the audience might be, and the idea of trying to sell someone on reading it seemed awkward. It reminded him of those poor women who worked in the fragrance department at Macy's, spritzing unsuspecting patrons with perfume. This was one area where he agreed with his mother. If these agents really gave a damn about discovering new talent, they wouldn't need someone's manuscript distilled into a letter, but would want to experience it fresh and make their own assessments. Kenny wondered, too, what if a writer described his book in a way that was all wrong, maybe the book wasn't about what he thought it was, but was about something even bigger that he hadn't considered? What if his own inability to recognize what he'd created prevented his manuscript from even being read, let alone published? Why can't literature, whether it's written by someone famous, or a hopeful unknown, be enjoyed like sex? Reading a book, thought Kenny, is like having the privilege of losing one's virginity anew, because each book is its own original event.

No, he wasn't going to play pitchman to an agent. He wasn't a salesman. He was a writer. He would send his baby to an editor. If he read it, fine. If he didn't, he'd move on to the next one.

Kenny thought about his lucky pen. It was still in its box, hidden in the back of his closet. He hadn't used it since he'd written *The Neon Bible*. He moved toward the closet door, then thought better of it. Instead, he pulled out a pencil and began to make a list of editors he'd been researching to whom he'd send his manuscript. The first was Robert Gottlieb at Simon & Schuster. Kenny had read *Catch-22*, which Gottlieb had edited. The satire was delicious to some readers and sophomoric drivel to others, and that's what excited Kenny. No one could agree. The reviews ran the gamut, too. *The Nation* and the *Herald Tribune* couldn't rave enough, while the *New Yorker* said it "gave the impression of having been shouted onto paper." Kenny wondered what Heller and his editor had thought when they saw that. The *New York Times* couldn't make up its mind: the first review praised the book, calling it "dazzling," while a later critique labeled it "repetitive and monotonous." Kenny imagined the meeting at Simon & Schuster when Mr. Gottlieb first presented it to his colleagues. Kenny had learned all about those meetings, and how books were chosen for publication. The meeting might consist of the acquisitions editor and the marketing, publicity, and sales directors. I bet Mr. Gottlieb had to fight for that book, Kenny thought, and he knew this was someone who would fight for him, too.

Kenny had researched everything he could about the history of *Catch-22*. It hadn't done well enough in hardcover to make the coveted *New York Times* best-seller list, even though it sold twelve thousand copies in the first few months. That seemed like an awful lot of books to Kenny, who imagined twelve thousand people jammed inside a stadium all reading the same work by the same author, and still it wouldn't be enough to satisfy the *New York Times*. Kenny realized he saw publishing through the wide-eyed idealism of a child and vowed he'd need to rid himself of his innocent notions if he were going to be taken seriously. Mr. Gottlieb mustn't know that I look up to him, Kenny thought. Besides, he reminded himself, the editor wasn't perfect. *Catch-22* only caught on after it was published in the U.K. and became a best seller there. Even then, Heller's masterpiece didn't find an audience in the States until Don Fine of Dell released it in paperback and the novel became a favorite among young adults and college students, for whom it resonated as a biting statement against the war in Vietnam. Kenny was fascinated by the idea of a book being a "cult classic." He hoped *Dunces*, that's what he'd started to call his book, would become one, too. He also thought, if Mr. Gottlieb didn't like his manuscript, I can send it to Mr. Fine, though he'd read somewhere that Fine could be mean-spirited. He got enough mean at home.

Kenny was in awe of Heller's resistance to literary convention. Kenny had been taught the rules of fiction writing, like the one about main characters, that they couldn't just exist, that they had to have a history, that they had to come from somewhere. Heller didn't follow rules. Neither did Virginia Woolf, another one of Kenny's favorite writers. When he read *The Waves*, Kenny was captivated by how Ms. Woolf intertwined poetry with prose, in much the same way he was drawn to Heller's satire, because both authors were courageous. That's why Kenny couldn't wait to send his contribution. Gottlieb won't be afraid to take a chance because that's what he's looking for, Kenny thought. Tomorrow morning, he would go to the post office on his way to the university. His heart beat excitedly.

It was an election year, but Kenny wasn't paying attention to the candidates. He took comfort in looking at the *New York Times* best-seller list every Sunday. John le Carré, Saul Bellow, Mary McCarthy. He imagined his name alongside theirs on the pages of the *Times*. For Kenny, writers were important and politicians mostly just rich fodder for amusement. He didn't much care for Lyndon B. Johnson and he liked Barry Goldwater even less. John F. Kennedy was the only one he respected.

Kenny worried whether his sense of humor, the way in which he'd mimic people, ever hurt anyone's feelings. He was aware that he had a tendency to go too far. He would see it on their faces. It was the same look his dad had when he'd suddenly realize he wasn't wearing any pants. Kenny never wanted to make anyone feel that way. Politicians and celebrities were fair game, but sometimes after he'd had a few drinks, he'd start impersonating someone whom everybody at the table knew. He'd realize he was being unkind, but he would get caught up in the moment. He wished there was a tiny time machine embedded in his watch, so that when he was mocking someone, he could push a button and undo it. He wanted to understand what made him that way, but his mother was not a fan of psychiatrists, telling her son that they were for the mentally ill, not for bright, talented young men like himself. His personality was to be celebrated, she'd say, not analyzed and dissected. Kenny assumed she knew best, as one of their ancestors was apparently certifiable. Thelma had never shared any details with him, other than thanking God the condition wasn't hereditary. Kenny wasn't so sure about that. Maybe he just enjoyed the attention. He didn't want to be cruel. And yet he'd find himself mocking people, telling himself that they understood it was all in good fun. Why did he seek attention that way? He wanted to believe it was because he loved to make people laugh.

When Kenny arrived at the post office the next morning, he handed his precious package to the clerk, proudly informing her it was for a famous editor in New York.

"Wait, are you sure I have the zip code correct?" he asked the clerk.

She grabbed a coffee-stained list next to the cash register and double-checked, reassuring him everything was in order. As Kenny watched her place his only copy of the manuscript in a large bin, he prayed, asking God to bless and protect Ignatius and guide him safely home to Simon & Schuster. The possibility that Simon & Schuster might not return the manuscript or that it could be lost in the mail never occurred to Kenny.

On the way to Dominican College, he stopped by his favorite café and ordered three beignets with extra powdered sugar, devouring them as Ignatius would. Then, ignoring the napkin neatly folded in his lap, he wiped his mouth with his hand, channeling his hero, willing his acceptance into the world.

Kenny had edited and reedited his work until his mind could take it no longer. He thought of Jack Kerouac, and how he never edited himself, that he allowed his stream of consciousness to fill his scroll. If Jack were in that café with him, he'd have told Kenny to leave Ignatius alone to let him exist in his pure, unexpurgated form, not tethered to grammar or rules.

Kenny was talking to Ignatius now, telling him to behave when he got to New York, to let the uptown editor get to know him as he did, and that in time, he would come to love and admire him in the same way. When Kenny got to class, his students were eagerly awaiting his arrival. He felt light-footed that morning. It was going to be a good day.

As the weeks turned to months, Kenny tried to not think about Ignatius. The atmosphere at home had deteriorated and, as Thelma's agitation intensified, so too did the expectations she placed on her son.

Kenny didn't know what was worse, the pressure he put on himself, or the subtle ways in which his mother could simultaneously lift him up and knock him down. During one of the psychology courses he'd taken at Columbia, he had learned about the Madonna-whore complex, something abusive men did, putting their women on a pedestal one moment, and then treating them like dirt the next. Kenny felt like that's what was going on at home, except that it was some bizarre dance between mother and son. He wondered if Thelma would see herself in the character of Irene Reilly, Ignatius's mother. To be sure, Irene was a kinder, weaker woman than Thelma, but she too could have a foul disposition. In those moments when Kenny was feeling uncertain, as if there were this stranger inside him that he couldn't control, he wondered if he had pushed Thelma to the brink. Sometimes when he felt alone, burdened by his mother's disappointment and stuck waiting for word from Mr. Gottlieb, he thought of Irene Reilly, and pretended she was his mom. And then he'd hear Thelma yelling from the kitchen, at what he couldn't fathom, it was the cadence of her voice, like a bug interrupting the tranquility of a windowsill.

By the end of the spring semester, Kenny had all but lost hope that he'd ever hear from Simon & Schuster, when the envelope finally arrived. The handwriting was precise and feminine. Definitely Palmer Method, he thought, as he mustered the courage to open it. It wasn't a thick envelope, which would have meant they were returning the manuscript. This appeared to be a letter. He didn't think it was a form letter either, as that would have been typed and not written in delicate cursive. He wished his uncle Arthur were visiting. Kenny would have asked him to read it first.

Kenny opened the letter. It was only three short paragraphs. He kept rereading it, unaware that he was giggling, until Thelma asked him through his closed door what was so funny.

"Nothing, Mother, just a letter."

Thelma opened the door and walked in, demanding to know what was going on. Kenny grimaced, wanting to savor this moment alone. He tried to ignore her but she wasn't having any of it.

"John Kennedy Toole, show me that letter this instant."

As Thelma read the correspondence from Robert Gottlieb's assistant, she shook her head disapprovingly.

"You'd think that having discovered such an important talent, this fellow would adjust his schedule for you and not expect things the other way around."

"Mom, he's an important editor, he's busy. I'm grateful he's interested in my work."

"Of course he's interested. Those who can, do, and those who can't, teach. Editors are like teachers. Do you think he could write such a brilliant masterpiece himself? His assistant should be offering to fly you to New York first class."

"Mother, why can't you just be happy for me?"

"And Mr. Gottlieb should be lucky to have you as a rising star at his publishing company," Thelma continued. "Call this assistant and ask that she book you on the next flight to New York, and to arrange a hotel. You don't need the Waldorf, but I've heard the Plaza is nice."

Kenny wanted to scream, but he was too delighted by the letter to allow Thelma to ruin his joy. Thelma, satisfied that she'd talked some sense into her child, whose humility wasn't going to get him anywhere in this life, finally left him alone and went to the kitchen to start dinner.

Kenny sat down and wrote a letter of his own, to Ignatius. He wasn't sure why he felt the urge to do this. He'd always kept a journal. It was something he found soothing when his thoughts became too loud for him to make sense of. A lot of people did that. The impulse to share the news about Simon & Schuster with Ignatius made Kenny wonder if he might be losing his balance. Then he remembered what his professor had told him, the same one who'd been helping him to understand how the publishing industry works. He told Kenny that the best writers hear their characters inside their heads, that their characters actually speak to them, even keep them up at night. Accomplished writers, he said, often complain that their characters never leave them alone. That's how Kenny felt. Sometimes he'd hear Ignatius, Myrna Minkoff, or Irene Reilly as if they were right there conversing with him. Kenny realized, after sending the manuscript to Mr. Gottlieb, that he was unhappy again, that working with the characters staved off a loneliness that he never discussed.

Though Kenny was always madcap, he felt separated from those whose admiration he inspired. He imagined it was not unlike what movie stars go through, not that he saw himself as a star of any sort. That was his mother. No, what he meant was that a movie star has the adoration of millions, but when they get home at night, they're alone. He thought about Marilyn and how even though fans worshipped her, she couldn't lean on any of them like a person. Fans weren't real in the way someone who loves you is real. Kenny knew Ignatius and his other creations weren't real, either. But he missed them. And so he kept writing to Ignatius.

He told him all about Mr. Gottlieb, why the editor was such an important man, and about the assistant's letter telling Kenny that her boss wanted to meet with him at his office in Rockefeller Center. He told Ignatius how nervous he was when he sent the manuscript, but that he couldn't let him and everyone else in their story down, and that he must persevere. He regaled Ignatius with details about the trip he was planning to New York later that month, and how Mr. Gottlieb's assistant had asked if he could come a few days earlier to meet the editor before he left for Europe.

Kenny knew that Ignatius wouldn't read the letter. He knew that, but he still grinned, envisioning Ignatius's expression if he did read it. Kenny thought to himself, he would probably rail against the establishment, start bellowing in the streets that Kenny was allowing his literary labors to be molested by mongoloids, and then, pointing his pudgy index finger in Kenny's face, command that he study Boethius or Batman to avoid succumbing to the horrors of optimism.

Kenny became so immersed in the letter to Ignatius that he didn't hear his mom calling him to dinner. It reminded him of when he was writing in his journal about Ginny, the lovely girl from math class, and how his mom interrupted that, too, announcing dinner was getting cold. He wondered how Ginny was. For a moment, he was tempted to call her and tell her about the letter from Simon & Schuster. He wasn't even sure if he had her number anymore. Such a shame, he thought. It was the last paragraph, only two short sentences, from the assistant, that he would have given anything to share with her: "Is now the time for me to tell you that I laughed, chortled, collapsed my way through *Dunces*? I did."

Suddenly, Kenny was starving. He couldn't remember ever being hungrier. When he ate dinner, his mother watched him devour two servings of stew, and then, after a rest, fill his plate again. Before she could comment, J.D. asked when she would be serving the chocolate cake. He distinctly remembered, he said, that she'd promised him cake. Sighing, she went to the cupboard, took out a chocolate MoonPie, and placed it before him. He said "thank you" with such sincerity that it almost broke her heart. By then, Kenny had used this opportunity to quietly exit the kitchen and return to his room.

Kenny had never felt courted before. He'd romanced only two people in his life, Ellen and Ginny. He realized that it would be prudent to maintain perspective and, like his uncle Arthur always counseled him, never believe anything until the money's in the bank, but Kenny couldn't help but be excited. He'd passed the first test. He'd awakened the interest of a top editor. Surely, he told himself, it would be easier from here.

Kenny didn't change the date for his New York trip to accommodate the editor's schedule. His mother had counseled him not to appear too eager, so he'd heeded her advice, choosing not to alter his plans, and missed seeing Mr. Gottlieb.

Years later, Kenny would curse himself for his stupidity. He did, however, speak to Ellen. He was surprised when she answered the phone, as he wasn't certain the number was active anymore. It had been five years since he'd seen her. She'd written him one letter, saying she missed him and that her parents had been asking about him. When Kenny heard her voice again, he felt like a nervous schoolboy. He talked about his life since Columbia, his teaching at Dominican, and his novel. He didn't say anything about Simon & Schuster. She told him of her new job working as a journalist at the *New York Times*. She said that her family had reluctantly accepted her desire to become a writer. Her father had been appeased by such a prestigious paper, and while he lamented her aversion to becoming a doctor and continuing his legacy, he'd come to terms with her decision. Kenny told her that he was going to be in the city later that month and asked if she'd join him for dinner.

The days passed quickly and soon Kenny was disembarking from his flight to New York. This time he could afford a modest hotel in Chelsea. On the cab ride from the airport, he thought about his long-ago sojourn to New York City with his friends from Tulane. Kenny guarded those memories, as his time at Columbia had soured him on New York, and he was hoping that this trip would reawaken his love for the place.

When Kenny arrived at his hotel, he was already fantasizing about what life would be like as a revered author. The letters, tucked neatly in his suitcase, were reassuring reminders that his destiny was finally within reach.

A few days after he received the initial overture from Mr. Gottlieb's assistant, he got a letter from the man himself, saying that he was sorry they'd miss each other in New York. Then the editor offered his appraisal of the manuscript. Kenny had read that part of the letter so many times, he'd memorized it:

"It seems to me that I understand the problem—the major problem—involved, but think that the conclusion can solve it. More is required, though. Not only do the various threads need resolving; they can always be tied together conveniently. What must happen is that they must be strong and meaningful all the way through—not merely episodic and then wittily pulled together to make everything look as if it's come out right. In other words, there must be a point to everything you have in the book, a real point, not just amusingness that's forced to figure itself out."

Kenny was disappointed that the editor saw anything wrong at all, but he recognized that Mr. Gottlieb had put his finger on the sore spot. Kenny wasn't used to criticism. Sure, he'd had a handful of professors in grad school review his work, and he'd have to do the occasional partial rewrite, but sometimes he felt it was because they gave him so many perfect scores. Their comments written in red pencil in the margins in tiny handwriting seemed apologetic, as if they had to stretch to find anything, whereas Mr. Gottlieb's suggestions resonated. Though he'd never admit this to anyone, well, maybe Ellen depending upon how much they drank later that night, Kenny had worried after reading Mr. Gottlieb's letter. He went through the manuscript hunting for examples of what Mr. Gottlieb had explained, trying to identify and fix them. It didn't come as easily as had his term papers in college. Kenny was determined to overcome his spoiled schoolboy self and be able to apply valuable advice, which is what this editor was trying to give him. It took Kenny only a moment to accept that maybe he wasn't as perfect as his mother insisted, but if he could let go of the grip she had on his opinion of himself, he'd be free to become who he was meant to be.

In the next paragraph of his correspondence, Mr. Gottlieb asked Kenny if what he'd written made sense to him. "I hope so," the editor said. "Because it's vital." Kenny recognized that if the man didn't believe in Ignatius and the book, he wouldn't waste his time with letters. Mr. Gottlieb had no obligation to Kenny. He wasn't a family friend who wanted to help or someone whom Thelma had cajoled, like the sponsors of her Christmas pageants. No, this was a stranger who received a manuscript and saw promise. Kenny had to learn to see his life through the mature lens of a grown-up and not the myopia of an overindulged child. Taking this manuscript and doing with it what the editor has suggested would not only prove a literary exercise, Kenny consoled himself, but it would be a leap toward the spiritual independence he desperately craved, but couldn't even articulate until he'd received the letter and began considering where he was in life and what he wanted for himself, not his mama, but his own Goddamn self.

Kenny still planned on visiting Simon & Schuster to meet the assistant. She had written Kenny a second time, asking him to let her know when he arrived. Kenny remembered how his dad had always treated the secretaries at the dealership with kindness and respect, explaining to Kenny that they often had the hardest jobs, being gatekeepers for their bosses, and if a man earned the respect of a secretary, he was more likely to earn the respect of the boss. Kenny dialed the assistant from the hotel and just when he thought she was gone for the day, she answered, expressing delight that he'd called. They arranged for him to come by the following afternoon.

Perfect timing, Kenny thought, as he was taking Ellen to dinner tomorrow evening.

EIGHT

John Kennedy Toole looked in the mirror. Not bad, he thought. He'd felt emancipated ever since he arrived in New York. He had money in his pocket and while he still couldn't afford dinner at the Plaza every night, he could certainly swing it this evening. John felt different this trip. No longer that struggling grad student, harried and uncertain of his future, John was comfortable with himself now. He knew what he wanted and what he needed to do. He would enjoy this brief respite in New York and absorb the energy of the city, but this time, instead of it making him feel as if no matter what he accomplished, or how hard he pushed himself, it would never be enough, he realized now, everything was different. John was in control and it would begin this afternoon at 3:30 P.M. at the offices of Simon & Schuster on Fifth Avenue at Rockefeller Center.

The assistant was looking forward to meeting the bright new talent that had created Ignatius Reilly. She was proud that she had pulled his manuscript out of the slush pile and taken it upon herself to vet it for her boss. There were stacks of submissions next to her desk, and why she chose that one in particular to read, she couldn't say. Perhaps it was the author's penmanship, the delightful symmetry of the loops, the way in which his upper-case *T*'s leaned to the right just so. Everything about the package he had sent, the label so carefully filled out, the freshness of the ink, the quality of the envelope, told her that this was a polite young man. He wasn't arrogant or entitled like so many aspiring writers, whose manuscripts she was responsible for returning with a vague but slightly encouraging rejection note. That the return address was marked New Orleans intrigued the assistant. When she began reading Mr. Toole's novel, the crude, gas-basket of a protagonist who, if she was going to be frank, she felt a little ashamed to find so funny, belied the apparent good manners of its creator. This was unexpected.

By the time she finished the book, she knew that Bob must see it. Though it wasn't what they usually published, he was always on the lookout for talent that he could introduce to the world. This thing might take some editing, she thought, but still, there was a raw, unapologetic quality to Mr. Toole's humor. The assistant could see a book like this causing quite the lively storm. She surprised herself with this sudden burst of daring, and wondered if it were possible for a fictional character to so infect a reader that the character's disposition was contagious.

As the assistant tidied her desk in anticipation of her appointment with Mr. Toole, the author was surveying his attire in his hotel room. He looked adult in his new pleated pants and blazer. He straightened his tie, checked his wallet, and made his way to the elevator. When the bell rang signaling each stop, he thought of the scene from *It's a Wonderful Life* where Zuzu, George Bailey's daughter, informs her father that every time a bell rings an angel gets its wings. Odd, he thought, that would come to mind, while descending floors. He certainly didn't believe in angels, unless he counted Mr. Gottlieb's assistant.

It was a beautiful day, unseasonably cool for late June, and John decided to walk. It felt ordained that he be back in the city. He wondered what his angel would be like. He thought she must be older. Her letters had a quiet confidence that someone less experienced couldn't feign. When they spoke on the phone, she was warm but reserved in the comforting tone of someone close to power. Even though he wouldn't be meeting Mr. Gottlieb, the assistant was a vital initial step. Though John had let Thelma and a couple of his buddies see a few pages of his manuscript, the assistant was the novel's first official reader.

When he arrived at Rockefeller Center, he stopped to admire the imposing bronze figure of Atlas, holding the world on his shoulders, and he imagined the day when he could stand at this same spot, look at that very same statue, and not feel a similar burden anymore, that all he'd ever dreamed about was coming true, that he was free, alive, and a published author, someone even his mother could respect.

One thousand three hundred and eleven miles away, in uptown New Orleans, an anxious mother was in her garden pruning the hibiscus. She tried to concentrate but her thoughts kept drifting to New York. She had been monitoring the time since early morning, following her son's big day from afar. She had even set all the clocks in the house one hour ahead to Eastern Standard Time so that she and Kenny would be in sync. It worked well, except for confusing her husband. Thelma Toole was busying herself as she did on most days when her child was away, until 3:25 P.M., when she realized her precious little boy was probably in the elevator at that very moment on his way to the publisher. She pictured him smoothing the front of his jacket, then reaching for his pocket comb and hurriedly running it through his hair. Was he wearing his new tie? He had complained when she first gave it to him that it was far too extravagant, but a mother knows her child, and despite Kenny's missives to the contrary, she could see by the way he went straight to the mirror and held it up to his chest that he was grateful. Burgundy with a delicate horseshoe pattern, the clerk at D. H. Holmes said it was the very latest style.

She wondered if he was the only one in the elevator or if he had company. She hoped it was the latter because Kenny would become anxious if he had too much time to think, and then he'd perspire profusely. No, a long elevator ride didn't sit well with his mother, not at all. Thelma hoped someone was sharing the elevator with her son, and that they were chatting about the lovely weather. She looked at her watch. There was dirt beneath her fingernails. Why had she forgotten to put on her gardening gloves? She picked up the pruning shears. The hibiscuses were uncooperative this year.

An hour later, she thought she heard the phone ringing and ran back into the house. J.D. was sitting in his chair, staring blankly at the newspaper in his lap.

"Can't you hear the phone?" his wife snapped.

She rushed to the kitchen to answer it. Within a few moments, Thelma returned to the living room, eager to share with her husband the wonderful news. J.D. was asleep. "There's no point in waking him up," she thought. She wasn't even certain he understood why their son had gone to New York. The day Kenny left, her husband had made him a cheese sandwich to take to school. She leaned over and kissed him softly the way she used to when they were first married, letting her lips linger on his warm, soft cheek.

⁂

John Kennedy Toole was whistling as he donned his new tie for dinner. He knew his mother had wanted him to wear it to his meeting earlier that day, but it went better with the suit he'd chosen for tonight. John was more nervous about seeing Ellen than he had been for his appointment at Simon & Schuster. He was pleased by how well it had gone. Though he wished he could have met Mr. Gottlieb, the assistant had a sharp wit and wry sense of humor that John admired. Even though they'd only exchanged a scant couple of letters and spoken on the phone briefly, it was as if they'd known each other before. They talked of their childhoods and favorite movies. They talked about the book, and the parts that made her laugh. At one point, John began mimicking Ignatius, bringing the chubby curmudgeon to life. The assistant was delighted by this impromptu performance, and found herself clapping as the author bowed and tipped his imaginary hunting cap to her. When John asked if she had any children, she said that she and her husband were hoping, but that it would be bitter-sweet, as she'd probably have to give up work and she'd miss this job. John frowned, and she must have noticed, because she immediately interjected that even if she did leave, Mr. Gottlieb was already excited about his writing.

John was so lost in his thoughts that he nearly forgot to take Ellen's gift. He had picked it up early that morning. Though he rarely wore cologne, today he made an exception, dabbing a small amount of Brut at the nape of his neck. He remembered when his dad had handed him the signature green bottle. He was getting dressed for his first date with Ginny and J.D. told him to put some on, that ladies found it attractive. John never shared with his father what happened that night, how Thelma had barged in on the couple at the movie theater. He was thinking of his dad as he got into a cab, wishing he could have been there this evening to see him off.

The bar at the Plaza was lively. Tuxedoed waiters were busy. He wondered if the activity in the kitchen was like a Three Stooges short, with cooks flinging chickens and caviar while a blonde B movie actress is getting chased around the room by someone named Curly who keeps saying, "whoop, whoop, whoop," as a flustered maître d' threatens to call the police, determined to catch these lawbreakers, jawbreakers, salt shakers, home makers, how Irene Reilly would have enjoyed coming here with Ignatius, his dear mother, oh dear, what if Myrna Minkoff walked in with her breasts spilling out of a sequined dress?

John's characters danced and frolicked in his head.

"Kenny, aren't you going to say hello?"

Standing in front of him, wearing a simple white summer dress, her hair falling loosely about her shoulders, wasn't the girl he knew, but the most beautiful woman he had ever seen. For a moment, he was paralyzed, just as he'd been in math class all those years ago, when the teacher asked him a question and he couldn't answer because he was too distracted by the pretty girl sitting in front of him. Kenny rose to greet her.

"Ellen, you're lovely."

Ellen smiled and hugged him. "I've missed you, Kenny."

Kenny helped her to her seat, then ordered a bottle of Chablis.

"I can't get over how grown-up you are," Kenny said.

"Being at the *New York Times* can do that to a girl."

"It must be a challenging place to work."

"It is, but rewarding, too. I've been on assignment. I had just got back when you called."

The waiter returned with the wine. He poured a small taste into Kenny's glass. It was cool and refreshing and reminded Kenny of summer grapefruit. "Thank you, it's perfect." The waiter filled their glasses.

For the next hour, Kenny listened as Ellen regaled him with the details. She told him about her trip to Mississippi, living in one of the Freedom Houses, absorbing everything she could about the movement that summer of 1964. Her editor wanted a feature about the young people heading there to teach in the schools. Most of them were white college students from affluent communities in the Northeast, putting their futures on hold to stand up for something many of their parents couldn't quite understand. Ellen was the ideal person for the job, her editor said, because she was the same age, same background, and fearless. The Mississippi Summer Project was news, and Kenny had been heartened by the stories of thousands of volunteers that included Jews and Christians, blacks and whites, poor and rich, all fighting for the rights of black voters. Kenny had been upset by the statistics. More than one-third of Mississippi's population was black, yet only seven percent of eligible black voters were registered. Some of the blacks that did succeed in registering were harassed economically, often driven out of their homes and businesses.

When Kenny first learned of the events unfolding in Mississippi, he had thought about going there to teach during summer break. Growing up in New Orleans, he'd seen how racism worked. He remembered his student Gator from SLI, and how grateful he was for an education. Sometimes Kenny would find himself smiling in the middle of a lecture because he'd look over at Gator, who would be listening with his whole body, leaning in, absorbing every word. None of Kenny's other students, even those who cared about learning, had Gator's fervor, that hunger to rise up and defy the prejudice that had stolen the light from their parents' eyes. Imagine, Kenny thought, having a room of students like Gator, who didn't see changing the world as an abstract concept but as something real and necessary. This wasn't just about Mississippi or even the South. Kenny felt a need to join the cause, to contribute. He'd telephoned the volunteer headquarters and had them mail him information. He still had the pamphlet. These weren't brick and mortar schools. Classes were held in churches and barns, on porches and under shady trees. Kenny would be able to teach students from perspectives outside academia. He would be giving them life lessons, helping them cultivate their skills as activists, providing them the tools to realize their destiny. He wanted to go, but Ignatius wouldn't hear of it. Kenny tried to convince Ignatius that he was wrong, that this would only be one summer, but to no avail. Kenny sighed. He was perfectly sane. This was what writers did. They became one with their characters.

"At first I was scared that I wouldn't be able to earn the volunteers' trust, but it happened so naturally."

He took a sip of his wine. The waiter returned, refilling their glasses. Kenny ordered another bottle even though the first was half full.

"I've heard some pretty wild stories about the Freedom Houses," Kenny said.

"The one I stayed in had about twelve people, mostly undergrads. Being there changed me."

"How so?"

"It was like everything we were taught by our parents never to do was happening in this house, and it was shocking and beautiful all at the same time. You know how our parents always had lots of hang-ups about sex and race?"

Kenny nodded.

"There wasn't any of that there. If you liked someone and you wanted to be with that person, you just would. Sometimes people would go with one person for a few nights, and then change partners, and there was no judgment or shame."

"It sounds like a hippie commune."

Ellen laughed. "Kenny, it was extraordinary to see all these people defying the hypocrisy that brought them there. They want their lives to mean more than their trust funds or their family's pedigree, or whether or not they'll get into Harvard Law or Princeton. They don't want to become their parents. So they've converged upon Mississippi, and in these Freedom Houses, they're loving and fucking and listening to Dylan, asking existentialist questions over peanut butter and jelly sandwiches."

"You should write your article exactly that way," Kenny said.

"And they could use someone like you, Professor Toole."

Kenny took this opportunity to tell Ellen about his meeting at Simon & Schuster and Mr. Gottlieb's letter, his interest in the book, why the editor was such an important man, and how he needed to spend the summer working on the manuscript.

Ellen was impressed. She told him the first time she submitted an article to her boss at the *Times*, that she was so nervous, she was tongue-tied.

"I agonized over every comma," Ellen said.

"And when he returned it?"

"He redlined almost the entire article. It was awful at first. But then, when I reviewed the edits and addressed them one at a time, it wasn't nearly so bad."

"Okay, but how do you know when to trust your instincts and not change something?"

"I think you have to listen to that voice inside that knows what it wants to say."

Great, thought Kenny. His voice was an ill-mannered, pontificating windbag with digestive troubles.

"Tell me more about the assistant."

"She doesn't have her own office, just a desk in an anteroom, so we talked in Mr. Gottlieb's office. The place was a mess. Manuscripts and books everywhere. At first, I couldn't even find a place for my coffee cup."

"I've heard that publishing houses are all like that, organized chaos."

"It was definitely chaotic. Apparently, the publicity department was having some sort of crisis when I was there, and this woman, I'm assuming she was the one trying to manage the crisis, kept walking in and out of the editorial department, shaking her head."

"Do you know what it was?"

"I heard her say something about John refusing to do the interview with *Time* and 'who the hell does that Brit think he is, for Christ's sake.'"

"John *Lennon?*"

In that moment, the enormity of having been at the offices of the same company who just published John Lennon's memoir hit Kenny.

"Kenny, are you okay?"

"I'm just realizing now how close I am to everything that has ever meant anything to me. What if I mess things up?"

"Stop thinking like that! You're brilliant and they will be lucky to publish your book."

"Now you sound like my mother."

"Then she's a very smart woman, because you are talented and one day I'm going to see *A Confederacy of Dunces* in every bookstore window, and I'll say, I knew him when."

Kenny smiled. "Speaking of bookstores, I got you something."

He handed her the package, neatly wrapped in parchment paper. Inside was a signed first edition of Simone de Beauvoir's *The Second Sex.*

"It was the book you were reading when we first met," Kenny said. "I remember how you liked to quote passages."

This was the sweetest, most generous gift she'd ever received. How could she have let this man go? She reached under the table and grabbed Kenny's hand. "How about we bring dessert to your room tonight?"

When Kenny returned to New Orleans, he again buried himself in the manuscript. Mr. Gottlieb had compiled a list of suggestions that Kenny was going through one at a time, trying to reconcile the editor's vision with his own. He was glad he'd made a clean copy for safe keeping. The process was arduous. Sometimes it seemed he was caught in the middle between Gottlieb and Ignatius, who were at odds more often than not over where this story was going. Gottlieb wanted order, continuity, a logical connection between the characters and events that propelled the narrative. Ignatius cried foul, baffled by the editor's inability to appreciate his godlike mind. Kenny was trying to appease them both, not to mention his mother, who couldn't understand why her child wasn't being paid for his labors.

"Mom, I've told you a thousand times, Mr. Gottlieb is doing me a favor. He's helping me make this thing publishable. I should be paying him!"

"What makes you think it isn't publishable already? Why are you relying on the opinion of one man?"

"I can't send it to anyone else. I have to see this through."

"I just think it's odd that an editor has you doing all this work, making you change this and change that, without having anything in writing."

"He's written me letters that prove he believes in me. He wouldn't do that if he weren't planning on publishing my book."

"If this editor believes in you so much, why won't he give you a contract?"

"Since when do you know about publishing contracts?"

"I asked the father of one of my music students. He wrote a book on the history of gumbo."

Kenny rolled his eyes.

"I told him all about your Mr. Gottlieb and he said that you shouldn't be doing anything without a signed contract and an advance. That's money they give you up front so you have something to live on while you're working on the book. I told him Simon & Schuster hasn't given you anything but instructions."

"I wish you wouldn't blather about my business to strangers."

"Kenny, something about this situation doesn't feel right." Thelma quietly closed the door and walked away.

It was a sweltering summer. Kenny continued to immerse himself in making his editor proud. There were moments, especially in the wee hours of the morning, after he had been hunched over the manuscript since breakfast, working and reworking, reading the revisions out loud so he could hear how they sounded, that his mother's skepticism began seeping into his head. Some nights when he finally would succumb to the urgency of sleep, it was often with his head resting upon his arms over the typewriter. It was as if he were pounding the nail until the hammer broke.

Meanwhile, Ignatius fumed, haunting his master's dreams. In one dream, Ignatius was selling hotdogs on Royal Street, when out of the shadows Atlas appeared, with the world still perched upon his shoulders, though his hands were gnarled and his body was bent over and shriveled. Suddenly, his eyes lit up like two yellow orbs in the center of his face, and he threw the world at Ignatius as if it were a mighty basketball, shouting, "Catch!" Ignatius ducked and the world smashed to the ground, shattering. Ignatius grabbed his hot dog cart, with the letters HELL emblazoned across the front, and shuffled off into the night. Kenny was sweating when he woke up. His neck and shoulders ached, and his bloodshot eyes stared into the darkness.

He tried to include some sort of balance in his life. He knew it wasn't healthy spending all day in his room toiling over the manuscript. Joel came to town for a weekend and he and Kenny visited old haunts, enjoying the French Quarter. Kenny had written Joel about the book, but he hadn't had a chance yet to tell him that he'd reconnected with Ellen. Joel was happy for his friend but concerned about the strain in his face. Kenny reassured him that it was just the pressure of revisions, but Joel sensed a deeper discontent, something lurking in the distance that would occasionally show itself, then retreat, tricking Kenny and those closest to him into believing all was right. Joel also noticed the edginess between Thelma and Kenny. He'd always liked visiting the Toole's, but this time he felt uncomfortable. Kenny's father had deteriorated significantly, and Thelma, who used to politely ask guests if they'd like to hear a song, now went directly to the piano, banging the keys and singing, her vocal cords desperately reaching for the music that was no longer within her command. The Toole household had always been peculiar, but there was joy nestled within its walls. Now that joy had been replaced by something synthetic and forced.

As the new fall semester began, Kenny eased into the routine of teaching. His reputation as one of the more engaging members of the faculty had grown, and there were waiting lists for his classes. He had stayed in contact with Ellen during the summer and they'd managed a weekend trip to Biloxi. It was the only time Kenny took a break from writing. Now that school was in session, Kenny felt more confident. He was sleeping normally and the cool autumn weather reinvigorated his senses. Adding to Kenny's lightheartedness was the completion of the rewrite. He was satisfied with his work and confident Mr. Gottlieb would be, too. It had been painful, making some of the changes, but Kenny trusted his editor. He sent the manuscript at the start of the semester. As days turned into weeks and he didn't hear anything, he grew concerned. He spoke to the assistant several times and she assured him that Mr. Gottlieb was simply busy with the fall book season, and that he was as enthused as ever about *Dunces*. By the time Thanksgiving arrived, Kenny's optimism was waning. Sometimes he managed to forget about *Dunces*, but it was temporary, and when he'd be grading papers or preparing a lecture, his mind would invariably return to Ignatius.

Then, just ten days before Christmas, it came. The letter from New York.

Kenny stared at the envelope. The address was typewritten.

The ink looked wet the letters were so black, suggesting to Kenny the ribbon had recently been replaced. He wondered if he was the first person to receive a letter typed with the fresh ribbon, and what that might mean. He had been searching for meaning in lots of things lately. If there was a rainbow outside, he'd conclude it was an omen that good things were coming his way, because rainbows meant *The Wizard of Oz*, and when Dorothy sings the song, she's singing about dreams really coming true, and seeing a rainbow couldn't be a coincidence.

Yes, he concluded, this envelope was typed with a fresh ribbon. It's a sign, just like that rainbow. He picked up the envelope and turned it over, examining the flap. He wondered who had licked the seal shut. Was it his editor himself or the assistant? Whoever did the honors had been precise, making sure every inch of the adhesive had been properly moistened so that the edges wouldn't curl open the way the edges of poorly sealed envelopes sometimes did. Kenny thought about the master of this envelope, that it must be a man because the job had a masculine quality to it. The address was directly in the center, not off to one side or crooked. This was the envelope of a confident person.

A banging on his bedroom door. Tentative at first, then more determined.

"Yes, Mother?"

"Let's see it!"

"I haven't read it yet."

A flinging open of the door.

"Give it to me, I'll read it."

Kenny shoved the envelope in his desk. "I will share it with you when I'm ready."

Thelma had never heard such an icy tone from her son. She remained in Kenny's room. Neither spoke.

"John Kennedy Toole, I did not sacrifice everything to raise a coward. Whatever is in that letter, be man enough to face it."

Silence.

Thelma went to the desk, retrieved the letter, opened it, and handed it to her child.

"You're not going to read it?" Kenny said.

She looked at him, as if making up her mind, then turned without a word and left.

Somewhere deep inside himself, Kenny believed his fears were groundless. He'd studied literature his whole life. He'd had the best professors at fine schools, who had prepared him for this moment when all of his hard work would pay off. *A Confederacy of Dunces* was unorthodox, but it was also a rich and colorful portrait of Kenny's version of New Orleans that was unlike any other. The adult man who was proud of his manuscript wrestled with the insecure boy inside who was afraid to open the envelope. Kenny unfolded the letter and began to read. As the editor's words sank in, Kenny felt something slipping out of him, something that he knew would never return. Page one, paragraph four, line twelve, this manuscript "isn't really about anything." That phrase kept repeating itself inside Kenny's brain. Not wanting to finish the letter but knowing he must, Kenny continued reading. "It wouldn't succeed; we could never say that it was about anything."

There was more, but Kenny couldn't bear to countenance. He had failed. He thought of taking his lucky pen out of the closet and using it to desecrate the manuscript. He would keep vomiting filth until the reservoir was dry and useless, as useless as he felt right now. Yes, he would take that fucking pen and write upon his face, his hands, his eyelids, anywhere he had exposed skin, and release his pain. "It's not about anything?" Kenny shouted. It's about *everything* and now it's gone. Kenny sat rigid in his bed, his characters all screaming at him. For a moment, he thought of burning Mr. Gottlieb's letter, but he was grateful to the man. He'd worked with him, put time and effort into his writing. He gave a damn about Kenny and this book, and now Kenny had disappointed him, the same way he always disappointed his mother.

The editor ended the letter with "Don't despair."

Kenny laughed.

He went into the kitchen, where his mother was making dinner, handed her the letter, and put on his coat.

"Where are you going?"

"Away."

Thelma knew better than to push. She wiped her hands on her apron, poured herself a sherry from the bottle she kept in the pantry, and read slowly. When she finished the letter, she decided to call the man. She dialed the number on the letterhead, listening to it ring, thinking about what she would say. She was surprised when a young woman answered. She could hear typing in the background. It must be the assistant, she thought. She tried to speak, then quickly hung up. It wasn't like Thelma Toole to retreat, but for the first time she wasn't sure what was best for her son. She stared at the phone, sipping more sherry, and phoned her brother.

"Arthur, this Gottlieb is so arrogant. He told my son that he had some agent read the manuscript, too. She agreed with him, and Kenny believes they couldn't be wrong."

"Why didn't Kenny try to get an agent in the first place, someone who would fight for him?" Arthur said. "Why in the hell was he doing all this rewriting without any sort of commitment? A good agent would have never allowed that to happen. They would have moved on to another publisher."

"Apparently, your nephew has inherited your stubborn streak," Thelma replied.

He wanted to answer back but refrained. It wouldn't help Kenny, and she'd called for advice.

"A friend of mine said his agent had negotiated with six, maybe seven publishers before they got a deal they could live with. How could Kenny let this man at S&S have such control over him?"

"Arthur, I told him I thought the whole thing smelled, that if this Gottlieb was so excited about his writing, he would have offered him a contract and then given him his edits. But Kenny won't hear of it. The more I push him to think about what's happening here, the more he resists."

"Did you call Gottlieb yourself?"

Thelma went silent.

"Come on, dear sister, I know you. Tell your brother the truth."

Thelma took another sip of the wine, leaned back into her chair, and did something she rarely ever did. She confided in her brother. She told him about Kenny's behavior, how he'd lock himself up in his room agonizing over the manuscript, trying to shape it to Gottlieb's vision.

"Every day, Kenny seems to be shrinking. A few times I stood outside his bedroom door, listening to him talking to himself. More than once I wanted to call that publisher. But then Kenny would never speak to me again."

Arthur listened to his sister. She was always so sure of herself and dogmatic. He once told a neighbor, after he'd had one mint julep too many, that his sister was like something out of a Tennessee Williams play. Thelma was irrepressible, and though they'd had some serious disagreements over the years, he loved his sister and understood that beneath her maddening behavior was a woman who was afraid she'd never measure up. Thelma's one chance at the greatness she believed she was born to achieve rested in Kenny.

"Sis, listen to me. We can guide Kenny but we can't protect him from reality. You've given him your opinion. I'll reinforce it because I agree with you, but it will be up to Kenny to make the decision."

"I called his office right before I telephoned you," she admitted. "A woman answered. I think it was the assistant Kenny met with this summer. I came close to saying something, but then I hung up. I want to help my child. But I don't know how. And you know what bothers me the most? At the end of the letter, after he informs my son his book won't ever succeed, that it isn't about anything, this after having him toil away for over two years revising it, wait, I'll read it to you."

Thelma continued. "'We know from experience that when . . .'"

"Who's 'we'?"

"That agent I mentioned, the one he showed Kenny's manuscript to. Her name is Candida."

"Candida *Donadio*? She's one of the most important agents in New York. She represents Mario Puzo and a lot of other major writers. Anyway, keep reading."

"'We know from experience that when Candida and I know something is basically for us, but not right, it is very difficult to have it right for other people in town on our wave length; and the others are out of the question.'"

"Can you believe that?" Thelma said. "Not only does he tell my son it's not for him, but he basically says, don't send it to anyone else, either. He's treating my Kenny like someone he's been dating for a while, doesn't want to commit to, but doesn't want him dating anyone else."

"Honestly, I think Gottlieb is sincere in his interest in Kenny's writing. I just think Kenny's work is so unusual, he doesn't quite know what to do with it, but also doesn't want to let it go. That's a difficult position for any publisher."

"You know I detest crude expressions, but 'shit or get off the pot' comes to mind."

She could drive anyone crazy, but he did love her dearly. After talking a few more minutes, Arthur promised to speak to Kenny about S&S to see if he could offer some help.

Later, when Thelma went to bed, sleep wouldn't come. She lay in the dark, praying her son was all right. At 2:00 A.M., she heard the door open and Kenny's footsteps as he made his way to his room. Thelma said a quiet prayer of thanks.

Kenny was drunk. He seldom drank alone. He didn't want to be home brooding, yet he didn't feel like company either, so slugging back a few Jamesons on Royal Street seemed like the perfect thing to do. Now his stomach was churning, his head was pounding, and all he could think about was crawling under the covers and shutting out the world. It was a week before Christmas and the French Quarter was alive with decorations. Kenny wanted to enjoy the holiday, but this year, he thought, he'd have to pretend. His father loved Christmas and would hide odd little gifts for Kenny throughout the house.

The next morning, Kenny made a decision. He would ask Mr. Gottlieb to return the manuscript. The man had offered and he'd accept. One of them had to let go.

Later that day, Arthur called and convinced Kenny not to do anything until after the holidays. After they spoke, Kenny took all of the letters from Simon & Schuster, placed them in a box, and put the box in the closet next to his lucky pen.

The holidays, though not joyous, were kind and patient. Arthur spent Christmas with Thelma, Kenny, and J.D., and even managed to make J.D. laugh at his jokes. It was as if the burdens each of them carried were on hold. Years later, Arthur would look back on this Christmas and wish he could relive it. He and Thelma didn't bicker. Kenny listened patiently to his father. The vestiges of discontent that permeated the Toole household were dormant, as if out of respect for the holidays.

NINE

ー∞∞ー

February 2004. The reporter stared at the phone. The woman hadn't sounded senile. That was the problem with chasing this story. Greeley felt like a detective obsessed with a cold case. So far, every lead he'd pursued created more questions than answers. It had been months since he and Professor Bell had lunch at the Knickerbocker to discuss the novel and its backstory. There were so many twists to this thing that just when he thought he had uncovered something stunning, another something would reveal itself. Exhibit: the woman he had just called, the assistant, the one Kenny had met in person. When she worked for Simon & Schuster and had given her boss Kenny's manuscript, it was June 1964. Assuming she was in her mid to late twenties at the time, that would put her in her late sixties now. Definitely not old enough for senility. Then why, he wondered, did he feel like he was entering a parallel universe trying to talk to her about Kenny Toole?

He wanted to ask her about a specific event that had apparently taken place somewhere between January 15 and March 5, 1965, when Kenny, after receiving a disappointing letter from Gottlieb that Christmas, decided to go to New York and confront him. The helpful library staff at Tulane had gone into the Toole archives and copied the correspondence between Kenny and Simon & Schuster. While a few letters appeared to be missing, there was enough that Greeley could start assembling the pieces.

Gottlieb's belief in Kenny's talent had been genuine and he wanted to help develop it, but the harder Kenny tried, the more both of them got lost. As a fellow writer, Greeley felt for Kenny, all those nights revising the manuscript, only for his hopes to be crushed in a single letter. Greeley sighed when he read Gottlieb's words, remembering his own attempts at becoming a published author, the rejection notices, and not wanting to accept that maybe he wasn't a novelist. Kenny's commitment was another animal. Greeley had read numerous letters when researching stories that he had worked on. It was commonplace for reporters to gather information from correspondence. The letters between Gottlieb and Kenny were different. There was an aliveness to them that made Greeley feel as if both men were in the room with him, listening, as he read out loud. It was a sobering exercise. Despite wanting to vilify Gottlieb, as several articles had done when *Dunces* was finally published, Greeley knew it wasn't that simple. Gottlieb was a luminary, someone who inspired respect, and Kenny, like many others before, sought to win that respect. Kenny had done that. The editor had not only dedicated time and energy to helping this unknown writer improve his manuscript, he'd encouraged Kenny and told him not to despair, that he'd always be there for him despite his uncertainty about *Dunces*, he was still rooting for him. That was more than Greeley had gotten from his own father when he'd asked him to read his manuscript. Weeks later Greeley found it still sitting on the nightstand, open to page five. When he asked him what he thought of it so far, the old man laughed and told him to stick to his day job.

No, Greeley told himself, Robert Gottlieb is not the bad guy here. He was constrained by the conventions of his industry. Corporate publishing had become more cookie-cutter than cutting-edge, and Gottlieb was braver than most. He'd discovered Joseph Heller. Gottlieb had sensed greatness in Kenny Toole, but Kenny couldn't see past that December letter. True, Gottlieb's words were harsh and perhaps he should have been more diplomatic, but what if Kenny would have hung in there, pushed through his despondency and kept writing? And if Gottlieb would have published *Dunces*, would his edits have made it a better book? The damn thing got hundreds of rapturous reviews and sold over two million copies anyway. Yet the ending really *didn't* go anywhere, and there were parts that seemed disconnected from the whole and without purpose. Greeley agreed with Gottlieb's letter and he felt for Kenny.

He wanted to fight for him, but what he was fighting for, he wasn't certain. Maybe figuring it out would help him come to terms with his own lost dream and the novel he'd abandoned.

The first conversation with the assistant had been perplexing. He had left a voicemail introducing himself, explaining that he was writing about John Kennedy Toole, and was hoping she could help him. The woman took a week to return his call. Greeley didn't find that unusual, as people could be ambivalent about talking to reporters. He considered the fact that she called back at all reassuring.

Years later, Greeley would recall the conversation differently. Selective memory would not allow him to accept she had lied to his face. Maybe she was just confused, perhaps the event he was asking about was so disturbing that her subconscious rewrote an hour of her life to protect her from something that might always haunt her. Greeley was not known for his tact when soliciting information from people. He believed that it was this very quality, his ability to put his humanity on hold just long enough to get to the truth, that would one day win him a Pulitzer. Greeley wasn't driven by ego. He was obsessed with truth, which is why he wouldn't revisit that phone call, as it would mean that he hadn't honored his journalistic imperative. No, with Gottlieb's assistant, something overrode Greeley's ethics, and it wasn't that she intimidated him. It was something he couldn't identify then, but one day, after everything was over and done, after his conclusions about Kenny Toole rattled New York publishing, would Greeley realize, whatever happened that day, he'd never find the truth. That would always needle him, but he wasn't aware of any of this when he finally got Gottlieb's long-ago assistant on the phone. All he knew then was that this woman sounded like something out of an old *Perry Mason* episode, her tone just friendly enough so that no one could say she was rude or impolite, but tinged with the imperiousness of someone who was hiding something, not just from the world, but from herself.

Greeley knew from the letters that Kenny hadn't seen Gottlieb that day. He was out of the office. Instead, Kenny had met with the assistant. Why was it that when Greeley asked her, she said she wasn't there, that the newspapers had gotten it all wrong? "I had left Simon & Schuster by then to have a baby. Kenny must have spoken with my replacement." Then she complained about how irresponsible those reporters were that had claimed it was she whom Kenny had seen. Yet when Greeley read the letters between Gottlieb and Kenny that referred to that meeting, both mentioned her name specifically. Why lie? Greeley had thought about reading those parts of the letters to her, but his instincts told him she still wouldn't budge.

The year is 1965. Twenty-six-year-old Peter Jennings becomes the face of ABC's evening newscast and the youngest anchor in television history. Activist Malcolm X is assassinated while President Johnson deploys the first U.S. combat troops to South Vietnam. Peggy Fleming wins the female figure skating championship as the Righteous Brothers' song "You've Lost That Lovin' Feelin'" reaches number one. Frank

Gifford announces his retirement from football for a career in broadcasting and Peter O'Toole takes home a Golden Globe for *Becket*. The month: February. The place: Manhattan, Rockefeller Center.

A young man who looks like Kenny Toole is standing beneath the statue of Atlas, his empty gaze fixed upon all the people coming in and out of the building from which he'd just emerged, and he is pondering what kind of day they are having. When he started out that morning, he envisioned cake and candles later in celebration of what he was certain would be a triumphant meeting. Instead, all he could think about now was using one of those candles to burn a hole through his brain so it would stop thinking just for one goddamn minute, because everything in his head kept getting louder and louder.

Yes, this man looked like Kenny, but someone else had replaced the spirit inside. Kenny had become a sliver of his former self, a disappearing act in the story of his own life. Although he tried to focus on one thought at a time, his mind was not right. For a moment, he was uncertain where he was or why. Lucidity had become elusive, making him wonder if he was really standing under the imposing figure of Atlas, hoping the statue would drop the world right on top of him and end his misery. Kenny wanted to scream but when he opened his mouth no sound came out. He wished he had learned sign language. If he had, he would climb that statue and give his rage release.

Kenny spoke through his characters and one of them in particular certainly hadn't lost his voice. He was ranting at his creator, spraying him with spit as he unleashed his vitriol. "Incompetent fool!" Ignatius bellowed. "Fortuna has castrated both our tongues because of you!" Ignatius began outlining his plot to overthrow the depraved kings of Simon & Schuster and their morally inferior minions who'd savagely turned on them. Kenny smiled sadly, realizing he would never have Ignatius's courage. He envied his progeny's bravado, the man's relentless commitment to the absurd that belied the genius beneath. Kenny aspired to be like Ignatius, someone whose belief in himself remained immutable, like the passing of time or the taste of fresh, cold water. Ignatius allowed Kenny to breathe when he couldn't use his lungs anymore. Every author of every book that sat in the windows of all those midtown bookstores, taunting Kenny like the kids used to do when he was in school, all of them were sucking his life away, except Ignatius, whose only animating force was their mutual survival. Ignatius's view of the world was like a kaleidoscope that revealed truth in colors no one recognized. Of course, Simon & Schuster would be afraid of those colors. Why hadn't Kenny realized that before, but no, he was too wrapped up in the excitement and awe of being published by a giant, and that giant had stepped on him like a piece of discarded chewing gum and he was stuck on the bottom of his shoe, and the giant simply kept on walking.

While Ignatius prattled on, Kenny pretended to be listening. How could he admit to his hero that he had no intention of mounting any sort of revolution, that he needed to put him, Irene Reilly, Myrna Minkoff, and all of his other beloved children back into the box inside his soul? For a moment, Kenny thought of *The Neon Bible* and he was strangely overcome with empathy for every child that had ever been miscarried and the mothers of those children. Kenny was facing the same agonizing loss. Mine would have been stillborn anyway, he told himself.

A small crowd had begun to notice the distraught young man wildly pacing underneath the Atlas statue, shouting at himself, like the drunken hobos in Washington Square Park. He certainly didn't look homeless. He was well-dressed, his shoes freshly shined. He was carrying his coat, which was odd, given how chilly it was outside, and down his back there was a large stain where he'd perspired through his shirt.

"Are you okay?" an elderly man asked.

Kenny couldn't hear anything except Ignatius, begging him not to put him in that box.

"Sir, do you need help?"

Perhaps it was the urgency of the stranger's voice that captured Kenny's attention, but as his mind began to clear, he realized how peculiar his behavior must have seemed. Kenny wanted to ask the stranger how long he'd been standing there, but he was embarrassed so he simply thanked the older gentleman for his concern and walked away. Kenny longed to be with Ellen, lay his head on her lap while she stroked his hair, reassuring him. He hailed a taxi and gave the driver her address, but as they arrived at her building he asked the cabbie to take him to LaGuardia Airport instead. On the flight to New Orleans, Kenny closed his eyes and imagined Ellen sitting next to him, holding his hand. He wasn't looking forward to returning home. He wasn't looking forward to anything anymore.

Greeley perused the letters again, searching for what went on in the assistant's office that February afternoon. Based on a long, rambling letter that Kenny sent Gottlieb afterward, Kenny had telephoned the editor, and that call hadn't gone much better than his visit with the assistant. Greeley could feel Kenny's rage spilling across the pages. Kenny's words were uncomfortably close to home. When Kenny spoke of his frustration with his life, how he had to choose between his family's financial survival and writing, how his characters were a part of him, that he couldn't give them up, but also didn't know what to do with them to earn Gottlieb's approval, Greeley remembered telling himself that his own manuscript had been rejected because he couldn't do his best work while struggling to pay his rent. He used his financial situation to keep from asking: What if his old man had been right and the writing simply wasn't there? Kenny didn't make those excuses. Hidden between the lines of his desperation was a need to be truthful with himself. Despite his vulnerable state, he had the courage to address his demons to the man he believed held his fate. Reading it, Greeley realized that John was brave in ways he envied. Then why, he wondered, didn't he send the manuscript to any other publishers?

Thelma knew better than to bother Kenny when he was writing. He hadn't spoken to her since he'd returned from New York. She could tell that it hadn't gone well. She tried to pull what happened out of him, but Kenny was cryptic. He barely acknowledged her presence in the house. He went to Dominican each day to teach his classes, then retreated to his bedroom the moment he got home. Thelma could hear the clicking of typewriter keys. She assumed he was laboring over that dreaded novel, that, as much as she believed in its potential, she hardly thought it was worth what her child was sacrificing. Kenny was young. There would be other books. "You have your whole life ahead of you," she'd try to tell him. "Let this go and move on," she'd say. Kenny would look at her as if she were a clerk in a department store trying to sell him a cigarette holder after he'd told her he didn't smoke.

Thelma could never tell him, but she had steamed open Gottlieb's last letter and read it. It was dated March 23, 1965. She remembered because that was a Tuesday, the day of her weekly garden club.

Thelma skipped garden club that afternoon.

Five days later she saw a letter in the outgoing mail addressed to the editor. It was tucked between the payment for the electric bill and a paper doll birthday card. The address was neatly typed precisely in the middle of the envelope, not too far to the left or right, straight and perfectly aligned, as if a ruler had been used to trace faint lines in pencil the way a child would, because neatness counted. Thelma was burning up inside.

———

Greeley rubbed his eyes. He'd gotten caught up in the back and forth between Kenny and Simon & Schuster. It was nearly midnight and he hadn't eaten since morning. He went to the kitchen still pondering. Toole's life was the stuff of a Broadway play. It was all there, the overbearing mother, the love story thwarted by time and fate, the dramatic backdrop of New York publishing, and the tragic hero for whom victory will come too late. Arthur Miller couldn't have invented a script with better bones, Greeley thought. After devouring a sandwich, the journalist sent a quick email to Professor Bell, updating his mentor and asking for a favor.

———

The Toole household hummed along, its matriarch assuming the burden of maintaining the false appearance of normalcy. If she only knew that her son wasn't laboring over that novel anymore, that he and Ignatius had decided that what they had was good, very good, and they were no longer going to subject themselves to unnecessary poking and prodding by outsiders.

Ignatius was delighted by this turn of events. Last time they were in New York, his creator was a sniveling, obsequious toad waiting to be transformed by a kiss, and now the goddess

Fortuna had intervened and imbued Kenny with a proper sense of theology and geometry.

John Kennedy Toole was exploring an idea for his new novel. He wasn't sure if it would take place in New Orleans or New York. He thought maybe he could take one of the characters from *Dunces* and build a fresh storyline. He had been refining the concept, exploring which character had the most potential. Ignatius already had too large an ego. No, he thought, it has to be someone who can handle the responsibility of a protagonist. He'd already filled several of his favorite composition books. It was the most fun he'd had in ages.

For inspiration, he decided to fly to New York after the spring semester ended. He also wanted to see Ellen. The evening he arrived, he took her to a lovely restaurant on Mac-Dougal Street, and though he wanted to unburden himself and confide in her about his last visit to the city, he kept the conversation light, chatting about a new book he was working on. She didn't need to ask what had happened with *Dunces*. Her lover's avoidance of the topic was enough.

By the summer of 1965, an outline for the new book was taking shape. John decided to resurrect the character of Humphrey Wildblood, who had been the original prototype for Ignatius. Humphrey, in this incarnation, would be a different fellow. John just liked the name and had always regretted not using it. He was developing Humphrey, leaning toward setting the story in New York. John remembered the colorful hobos of Washington Square Park, how they'd fascinated him. He wondered about their lives, how they ended up sleeping on benches, each with their own vibrant spirit. He thought about their mothers and fathers and sisters and brothers. Where were they? What had happened that they let their loved one languish in a public park in a large city all alone? Or perhaps they didn't know. Every one of those people had a story. John Kennedy Toole wanted to take one of those characters and unravel that story. Yes, his name would be Humphrey Wildblood. Kenny was excited. It was like adopting a puppy after a beloved old dog dies.

Ignatius fumed. He hadn't had any contact with his creator since March. This was unacceptable. And now the man was in New York, spending time with that girl Ellen. He didn't even like the way the woman's name felt on his tongue, *"Ellen."* Ignatius let out a grunt. Communist whore, he thought.

Kenny never used to mind the muggy weather in New Orleans, but this year he felt suffocated. After he got back from New York, he grew increasingly restless. He was still working on the new book and Ignatius was terrified he'd be forgotten, trapped inside the pages of a manuscript that was sitting in a box, never to be published. Each day, Ignatius waited to be let out, his anxiety turning to despair. Ignatius felt responsible and was determined to help both author and protagonist escape their prison. Late at night, Ignatius ruminated, consulting his dog-eared copy of the *Consolation of Philosophy*, hoping Boethius could illuminate a way out. His chubby fingers appeared elongated, graceful, as he slowly turned the pages of his book, defying the limitations of his character, becoming his own man. In the sweltering heat, from the confines of a dark closet, the spirit of Ignatius Reilly abandoned the story from which he'd been born, vowing to never be a writer's puppet again.

Meanwhile a frustrated Kenny was trying to endure yet another lecture from his mother on why he should finish his PhD. He hadn't slept well. Ignatius kept waking him up in the middle of the night, begging to be released. It was so bad one night that he got out of bed, opened the closet door, and shouted at him to be quiet. The next morning, he convinced himself it had been a dream.

As the summer slipped into autumn and New Orleans became bearable, Hurricane Betsy tore through the South. Except for Thelma's beloved garden, the Toole family was fortunate. Their neighborhood was spared. In other parts of town, the flooding was so severe that people drowned in their homes. Though Thelma tried to tell herself that she should be grateful that all they lost were some flowers, it was as if a piece of her soul had been torn out. As she surveyed what remained of all those long hours creating life, now flattened by a single act of God, she suddenly felt a piercing pain, because in that moment, with sirens screaming in the distance and the television blaring as her husband stared blankly at the screen, Thelma Toole understood what her Kenny felt, not wanting to let go of his book. She wished she could erase all the horrible things she'd said to him; that he was weak and when did he plan on becoming a man. She had even called him a failure. How could she have called her beautiful little boy that awful word? When he told her that he wasn't upset with Gottlieb, she couldn't remember all she'd said, except this: "You're such a disappointment."

Kenny had been trying hard to prove to his mother she was wrong. One evening, he was watching the local news. For him it was a guilty pleasure. The national news was trustworthy. Kenny had taken journalism classes at Columbia and had great respect for the Edward R. Murrows of the world. The local news was mostly foolishness, plastic-coated anchors trying to pass off insipid dribble about some regional beauty pageant or a talking cat as events of importance. Once in a while, Kenny would watch with his dad keeping him company, and would enjoy the occasional salacious gossip about this congressman or that debutante, but as far as reliable news events, Kenny preferred the *New York Times*. However, on that particular night, Kenny found himself staring at the television, unable to look away.

Apparently some controversial publisher in Greenwich Village called Grove Press was releasing a long-lost romance novel written by Jean Harlow, titled *Today Is Tonight*, that had the entire staff of *Mademoiselle* in tears. Jean Harlow had been dead for over thirty years. The literary critics were panning the book, labeling it amateurish, yet it was acclaimed as the most enjoyable book of the season. Kenny was happy for Jean Harlow. He loved her old movies. He'd seen *Dinner at Eight* three times. Kenny always wondered if Jean Harlow had inspired Marilyn Monroe. Kenny didn't know much about Jean Harlow, other than she had a complicated, strained relationship with her mother. Ironic, Kenny thought, that based on what he was hearing in the news report, it was her mother's relinquishing of the literary rights that had ultimately led to the publication of her daughter's novel.

Kenny recalled a recent *New York Times* article. He went to his bedroom and began rummaging through his pile of the Sunday *Times*. He found the article almost immediately. The headline read: COMING! JEAN HARLOW IN HER MOST ROMANTIC ROLE! He read Richard Lingeman's tongue-in-cheek review of the book. Though Lingeman castigated Harlow the twenty-four-year-old author as campy and called her writing "untrammeled romantic fantasy" the tone of the review belied a certain awe about Harlow, not who she was, but what she wished she could be. It wasn't Harlow's writing that mattered, Kenny realized as he finished Lingeman's piece, it was the immortality of her heroine.

Kenny experienced an unexpected sense of relief. Perhaps what had happened with *Dunces* wasn't a failure, but a delay. What if he were to die too young like Harlow, and Ignatius lived on years later? It was an unlikely notion, he realized, but it brought him solace. Kenny had pondered fame, but never considered posthumous glory. He had honored van Gogh, Emily Dickinson, Baudelaire, and others like them, whose gifts weren't appreciated until long after they were gone.

While Kenny daydreamed, thousands of miles away a young man was continuing his drive across Europe in an old diesel Mercedes he'd purchased for a couple hundred bucks. This fellow had two thousand dollars in his pocket that he'd calculated would last him at least ten months, if he stayed in hostels and behaved sensibly. After leaving college, he had spent two years in West Africa in volunteer service and learned a good deal about diamonds, their value, and the ways they can be smuggled. And so Kent Carroll, who would one day hear Ignatius's cry to live as clearly as had John Kennedy Toole, kept on driving, contemplating the life ahead of him as only someone that age could envision.

What he didn't know then, when he stopped for a cup of coffee and to read the newspaper, and as he began skimming an article about Jean Harlow's novel, was that only a few years later he would be the editor of the house that published it. All this young man knew then was that he wanted the future, not the past.

In that moment, another young man, equally destined, had the same thought, only he wasn't sitting in a café, he was lying awake in bed, unable to sleep because someone named Ignatius wouldn't leave him alone.

TEN

The last letter from Simon & Schuster arrived in January and marked the final exchange between Robert Gottlieb and John Kennedy Toole. By then, Kenny had already moved on and was planning something else. It would require patience and sacrifice, but what noble endeavor didn't?

Ignatius had finally shut up and was making an effort to control his unfortunate behavior. Kenny had explained to him that he was working hard for their future and that he had to trust him. Ignatius had grumbled at first, but there was a fire in his creator's eyes that he'd not seen before, so he found himself believing in him again and his vow to secure their place in history.

It is 1966. Pampers introduces the first disposable diaper. Miniskirts are ubiquitous, punctuating the bold, new spirit of America's youth. Hundreds of thousands of protesters stage anti-Vietnam rallies across America, and Muhammad Ali, formerly known as Cassius Clay, declares himself a conscientious objector and refuses to go to war. Ronald Reagan becomes governor of California, while Simon & Garfunkel release *Sounds of Silence*.

Kenny got through each day the same as he did the day before. He awoke at precisely 6:00 A.M., endured the necessary pleasantries with his mother, followed by a kiss on the cheek and a promise to make her proud. Then he'd walk to Dominican, where he'd teach the same class, every day, to the same girls, most of whom were wearing the same pink lipstick and the same store-bought eyelashes.

There was one student Kenny favored, a lit major named Eva whose father was a police officer in Biloxi. She was eager and earnest and took copious notes. She wanted to write stories, perhaps novels. She admired Professor Toole, a fact Kenny was not entirely unaware of, and it made going through the motions every morning at home that much more bearable.

Eva, what a lovely name, he thought. It wasn't that Kenny had romantic feelings for her. He was true to Ellen. It was her innocence, intelligence, and adoration that sustained him each morning before he left the house, and the ritual to which he succumbed to maintain peace. At least he didn't have to pretend to have lucid conversations with his father anymore. J. D. Toole would smile occasionally and say hello, but he was in a perpetual dream state, the way some say a spirit is when they haunt a house, going from room to room confused, unaware that they're dead.

Thelma had been touchy the past few weeks. It was odd, he thought, how his mother tried so valiantly to keep things from him. He marveled at the irony. On one side, she treated him like he was a child, protecting him from things she thought might be upsetting, yet she seemed indifferent to her son having no private life because he was her everything as well as the breadwinner. You can't have it both ways, Mother, he'd mumble to no one in particular. I can't be your little boy when it's convenient, and then suddenly, I'm the man of the house! Kenny was becoming easily distracted. He'd be focused on one thought, his mind would go somewhere else, and by the time he wound his way back to the original thought, it would disappear. Touchy, Thelma had been touchy, yes, because of the incident with her brother George.

Kenny didn't know much about his uncle George. He recalled meeting him when he was very young, and that he talked to himself, but not like most people did, when they didn't think anyone could hear. He'd blurt things out loud, in a crowded room, making everyone uncomfortable, a condition that years later would likely have been diagnosed as Tourette's syndrome. Kenny thought it was hilarious. Thelma was embarrassed and whenever Kenny would ask about his funny uncle, she would stare him into silence.

Uncle George had become too much of a burden on the family, and Uncle Arthur had asked the state to have him institutionalized. A white Cadillac came to take him away to a place called Charity Hospital. Kenny understood the part about his being a burden. Certainly, his own father belonged in an asylum. It was the idea of it that bothered him, that someone suffering from an illness that isn't their fault could be legally kidnapped and subjected to the horrors of a psychiatric ward for the rest of their life. Ignatius's circumstances weren't all that different, Kenny thought. Ignatius's own mother had finally come to the conclusion that he belonged in a place like that, too. The final scene in *Dunces* almost seemed a premonition of what Thelma and Uncle Arthur were planning for their brother. Thank God, Kenny said to himself, that he'd had the presence of mind to ensure Ignatius's glorious escape from such a fate.

Kenny wasn't sure if he believed in God or not, but he wanted to. The idea that the existentialists might be right, that the burden of freedom puts each man at the helm of his own destiny, and that life has no meaning other than what an individual creates for himself, was terrifying. He found comfort, not so much in religion, which he considered fraught, but in having faith in something larger than himself. Kenny liked thinking there was a God who actually listened when he prayed, an act he didn't do often, and knowing that a heavenly father, one that didn't forget to turn off the stove or who talked to doorknobs, was there to protect him. Kenny also wrestled with his faith. The last time he and Ellen were together, they read to each other from the works of Descartes, Kierkegaard, Sartre, Nietzsche, and other philosophers they'd discovered in college. They sat Indian-style on the bed, sipping Bordeaux from the bottle, and shared their favorite passages, discussing their meaning. These conversations stirred Kenny's soul and imbued these iconic thinkers with a romantic allure more enticing than any sixth-grade Bible study class. There was one quote in particular from Kierkegaard that had captured Kenny's imagination. "The thing is to understand myself, to see what God really wishes me to do: the thing is to find a truth which is true for me, to find the idea for which I can live and die."

Kenny knew that he was different from his parents and even his friends. He was too polite to say this out loud, though if he had met Søren or Jean-Paul at one of those wonderful taverns in Greenwich Village, or perhaps on a long train ride from Prague to Paris, he would have admitted that what hurt him most was that he was aware of his talent and that all these other writers being published by big New York houses didn't have more than he did. If there was something wrong with his ability as a writer, if he thought he didn't have what it takes, he could accept *Dunces* gathering dust in his closet. But John Kennedy Toole understood that he had a gift. It wasn't that he was full of himself, he was simply proud of Ignatius and the other characters that he'd created whom he'd come to love like children. He had long forgiven himself for *The Neon Bible*.

As winter cast its heavy, gray blanket over New Orleans, Thelma sensed her son retreating. It wasn't anything specific that he said or did. She had grown accustomed to his mood swings and the way he'd cocoon himself in his room for days, barely speaking to anyone. She had come to accept these long stretches of sullen behavior as part of his eccentric genius, common among writers of her child's caliber. Thelma had done her research. She'd read about Tennessee Williams, Ernest Hemingway, and others, who were even more difficult to bear than her son. Kenny knew his mother was worried, and if he wanted any peace for either of them, he'd have to fake it, so he pretended his work was rewarding, and he pretended to be excited by his recent promotion at Dominican, and he feigned exuberance the day he moved his family to a desirable apartment on Hampson Street, with the loveliest garden on the block. Not everything was an act. When he surprised his parents with a new color television set one Saturday afternoon and saw his father's smile and Thelma looking so proud that her son could afford such an extravagant gift, Kenny felt content.

By the spring of 1967, Kenny had become skilled at convincing everyone he was fine. Occasionally, he'd hear Ignatius sigh or feel his fat, determined fingers poking at his ribs, but he'd made his hero a promise. The old gasbag would just have to be patient. Kenny suspected it was the new novel distressing Ignatius. Kenny had tried to explain that he needed the creative outlet to preserve his sanity, and more important, once Ignatius was famous and readers were clamoring for the next book, it would be immediately available. Kenny was growing annoyed with Ignatius. He decided that maybe he didn't want kids. If they were anything like Ignatius, it would be exhausting.

Kenny was eager for the semester to end and summer to commence, offering a respite from grading essays and planning lectures, and a chance to catch up on his reading. He'd finally begun Jean Harlow's novel. Ever since he saw the review months earlier in the *Times*, he'd been thinking more about writers whose books didn't become famous until after they died: Keats, Poe, Dickinson, Melville. There was so much he wanted to ask them.

The morning of the summer solstice, Kenny received an invitation to visit Wisconsin from his old army buddy David, the fellow who'd given him his first typewriter. David lived in Madison, a university town that intrigued Kenny. He'd learned that a professor and a group of students had staged a protest that drew five thousand supporters and nearly brought the city to a standstill, all over a disagreement about a wrong-way bus lane. If Kenny hadn't known better, it could have been Ignatius inciting the crowd. He could see it, Ignatius in full battle attire, wielding his sword, directing his flock to overthrow the gods of chaos and lunacy who were cunningly disguised as bus drivers and secretly plotting against the university. Kenny chuckled to himself and then immediately regretted it, as it awakened Ignatius.

"When do we leave for Madison?" he asked.

"I'm sorry, but I'm not taking you with me."

Ignatius's lower lip trembled.

"Don't try and make me feel guilty. I told you, you have to be patient, and I need a break from everyone right now."

"Are you going to work on that other book when you're there?"

"No, I simply want to enjoy a weekend with an old friend."

"But I'm your best friend!"

Kenny closed his eyes and willed his mind to be silent. Then he went to the bathroom and splashed cold water on his face.

The trip to Madison was a welcome change of pace, except for one small problem. His protagonist was a clever stowaway.

Kenny felt at peace during the flight and napped fitfully for most of it. When he saw David smiling and waving to him at arrivals, he forgot about New Orleans, work, his parents, and the manuscript in the closet. He even managed to put Ellen in perspective. After all, they lived in two different parts of the country, and although he thought he might love her, in fact, he was almost certain that he did, he was also acutely aware of everything weighing him down, including missing her. That weekend he gave himself permission to be young again and was looking forward to good conversation, flirtatious coeds, and drinking until he'd had his fill. Suddenly it struck him, when did he start thinking of himself as old? He hadn't yet turned thirty.

He started in the first night. David and Kenny were on their way to a popular bar when David saw a friend he wanted to introduce to Kenny. Kenny was too distracted to notice. Ignatius was insisting they go to the drugstore across the street because he was once again experiencing intestinal distress. Before Kenny could tune Ignatius out, he was halfway to the pharmacy. Kenny never noticed the perplexed expression on David's face, who couldn't understand why his guest had behaved so rudely. David also wondered why Kenny kept talking to himself all evening. He wanted to ask Kenny what was going on with him, but by the end of the night, given their mutually inebriated state, he thought it better to just let it alone. Everyone has their quirks.

When Kenny and Ignatius returned from Wisconsin, Kenny buried himself in the new book. It didn't come alive like *Dunces* had, and his main character, Humphrey Wildblood, the hobo from Washington Square Park, felt forced. Though Kenny had lived in New York, he wasn't *of* New York. The humor that had come so effortlessly when he wrote about New Orleans didn't avail itself this time; there was an inauthentic quality to it that made the author uncomfortable, like kissing someone you barely knew. Kenny simply wasn't connecting with Humphrey Wildblood. Books are like children and some writers, like some parents, are only meant to have one because that child is so extraordinary another isn't necessary.

As Kenny's frustration grew, so too did his concern that maybe one book was all that he had in him, like those musicians who have one song on the Hit Parade. What if *A Confederacy of Dunces* was that one song for him and no one would ever hear it? The more this worry took hold, the more his fascination with posthumous fame deepened. It wasn't that he harbored some macabre desire to achieve celebrity through death. It was something else that he couldn't explain, as if he felt a pair of invisible hands on his back guiding him. These were heavenly hands, the kind that his mother told him about when he was a little boy, and how he never had to be frightened because his guardian angel was watching over him.

It made Kenny angry that some of these dead authors who never got to enjoy their success were labeled mentally ill decades after their passing. Who's to say that their illness wasn't their gift? Would Emily have penned those gorgeous poems had despair not been her muse? Imagine, thought Kenny, if Gregor Samsa had turned into a unicorn instead of a cockroach? Kafka's morose interpretation of the human condition was as much a window into his genius as it was his infirmity. He wondered if there was a fraternity in heaven for the great writers and poets throughout history, and if you had to be published to get in or if they'd make an exception if they liked your work. Many of those authors died thinking they'd never be acknowledged. History would see them differently. Kenny wished he could invite every one of these people to dinner, and he'd have a huge movie screen where he'd show the films that were made of their books, the lectures in their honor, and tourist attractions to commemorate their lives. He'd talk about the universities that offered entire courses on their work. He'd hand them copies of all the biographies that were written about them and the encyclopedia entries that went on for pages.

In early November, Kenny invited David to New Orleans for the weekend to reciprocate his kindness. He asked his mother to keep his dad out of sight. Though a part of Kenny felt guilty, he was tired of having to explain J. D. Toole to visitors. Kenny was on edge. At first, he thought it was the last-minute rush grading midterm exams that had caused his anxiety, but the rational part of his brain knew something had occurred. He could feel it sucking the levelheadedness right out of him. Between Ignatius's bugging him, his mother's incessant peck, peck, pecking at him, his father's vacant eyes, Ellen's wanting to know when she'd see him, and his students' making fun of him behind his back—and he knew that they were because he could overhear their conversations, it was as if he suddenly had extrasensory perception and he could see and hear things that had previously eluded him. And the noise in his head kept getting louder.

Kenny didn't give his guest a chance to unpack or change his clothes. He whisked David from the airport, dropped off his bags, then informed him they were going on a VIP tour of the Quarter. David thought his friend seemed off, but after their previous visit together he had convinced himself that Kenny was just eccentric and that lots of writers were that way. It wasn't until they pulled into a cemetery and Kenny announced that this was their first stop and he had something very special to show him, then proceeded to trudge through the cold, damp graveyard, stopping at the Toole family mausoleum, did David realize that something was amiss. Though the above-ground crypts, a necessity in New Orleans to avoid caskets being washed away by floods, were often a draw for tourists, Kenny's joy in this gloomy place alarmed David, who in that moment was wishing he was on an airplane headed back to Madison. When Kenny suggested they stop at the Old Absinthe for a drink next, David's exhale created a tiny breeze. As they were winding their way down Bourbon Street, David noticed Kenny growing fearful. He asked him what was wrong, to which Kenny mumbled something about outsmarting the little vixens. David had no idea which vixens he was referring to, but thought perhaps he meant the group of girls exiting the bar, who appeared to be having some sort of bachelorette party. One of them was wearing a veil, the kind you'd find in stores that sold Mardi Gras beads and paper hats. David started to put a hand on Kenny's shoulder to dissuade him from interrupting their fun, when suddenly Kenny turned and walked toward the alley. David followed behind him, wondering what was going on.

"They won't leave me alone," Kenny whispered.

"Who? I don't see anyone."

"My students. There's a group of them that follows me all the time and they laugh behind my back."

David, unsure what to say, put his arm around Kenny's shoulders.

"Shall we quench our thirst buddy? I'm certain they're gone by now."

The next morning, Kenny was awake by 6:00 A.M. and already packing snacks for the ride. When he told David about the trip to Biloxi he had planned for them and asked if he was ready, David reluctantly agreed. Perhaps it would give him an opportunity to find out what was happening to his friend. As they loaded a cooler and beach towels into the trunk, David wondered if he was overreacting, as Kenny now seemed fine.

On the way to the beach, they took a detour by the Biloxi River. Kenny turned onto a dirt road that snaked through the backwoods. The only signs of human life were a handful of ramshackle fishing cottages and what was left of an abandoned one-room schoolhouse. The landscape reminded David of something out of *Grimm's Fairy Tales*, a labyrinth of ancient trees, their great muscled limbs twisting upward toward the sky. Kenny rolled all the windows down and breathed in the scent of fertile earth, pulling it into his lungs, then exhaling long and slow, as if he were dragging on a joint. Now David was reminded of those old gangster movies he used to love as a kid, where the hitman lured his unsuspecting victim, usually someone who knew and trusted him, into his car for a "road trip," then made the guy disappear. I'm being ridiculous, David thought, but as they descended deeper and deeper into the woods, he began to worry, not for himself but his friend. They kept on driving until the road dead-ended at a bog with a view of the water. David had lost his bearings and asked Kenny why he had brought them there.

Kenny got out of the car and motioned for David to follow him. They walked for about ten minutes, until Kenny stopped beneath a sprawling oak tree, the kind with roots that seem to go on forever, with gnarled branches and lush, green leaves. The tree had an eerie, almost human quality to it. They were both wearing sandals and their feet were covered with mud. David remembered Kenny as always so fastidious. He didn't even like his galoshes getting wet.

"Where are we?" David asked.

Kenny smiled. He had a look in his eyes as if he were watching something unfold that no one else could see.

Nearby, a heron took flight, the whoosh of its wings interrupting the stillness.

———

Location: New York. Time: A frigid, cold February morning, 1968. The offices of Simon & Schuster were bustling. Publicity assistants were gathering media reports, assembling press kits, and scheduling interviews for their author George Deaux, whose third and most anticipated novel, *Superworm*, was being released that day. Robert Gottlieb, the book's editor, was leaving the following month for Knopf, and this would be one of his final titles at Simon & Schuster. He wanted his departure to end on a success.

The author's previous work had launched to mixed reviews. Deaux understood what was at stake. When an editor moved on to another publishing house, the authors whom they'd nurtured and developed were often left without a champion. Good editors did much more than editing. They fought for their books, shepherding them through the publishing process, making sure they were supported by the other departments, all the while shoring up their authors' resolve.

Later that same week, another writer in another town, one with milder winters and larger gardens, was still in the café he'd stopped at hours earlier, hunched over the book he'd purchased on his way to work. He'd ordered coffee and beignets, both of which remained untouched. The owner of the café was getting ready to close and had politely asked the man to leave.

He dismissed her entreaties with a flourish of his wrist, saying something about downward spinning wheels and cheese dip. She considered calling the police, but she'd seen this customer before and he was always kind and polite. In fact, if she didn't know better, she would swear the person sitting at that table simply bore a striking resemblance to the well-dressed young man who always complimented her beignets.

"Is there something I can help you with?" she asked.

The man grinned at her: "Capricious sprite, she has ruined all our fates!"

The café owner hesitated, uncertain what to do, when Kenny closed the book, thanked her for not calling the authorities, and walked out the door. In the years to come, she would look back on the odd encounter and wonder why she wasn't afraid. Perhaps it was the way in which the man hung his head when he left, his tired, bloodshot eyes revealing a pain so sharp that it seemed to have carved lines in his face. Whatever was in that book had upset him, and it had such a strange name: *Superworm*.

Ignatius was growing weary. Preventing his creator from succumbing to despair was demanding. Donning a jeweled crusader helmet that he kept hidden under the bed in his Howdy Doody pillowcase, the indomitable Ignatius Reilly prepared himself for the battle of his life.

Meanwhile, John Kennedy Toole got through each day the same way he had the day before, stuffing down his anger at the world, believing that God would give him the courage to complete his plan when the time was right. When Martin Luther King Jr. was assassinated just before Easter, Ignatius felt the oxygen drain out of his creator. Ignatius didn't know who the dead man was or why he, too, felt sad that he'd been killed, but that night the bedroom on Hampson Street had never been as quiet.

Summer came and went. Kenny didn't visit Ellen. She finally convinced him to let her come to New Orleans so they could spend a few days together. She went back to New York the next morning. Years later, Ellen's granddaughter would recall the sadness in her nana's voice whenever she talked about the wonderful young man who'd been her first love, and their last night together. "Nana told me he was mean as barbed wire and that she couldn't bear it because he'd always been so kind and loving. It was as if he had become someone else."

Thelma was worried to distraction. She did everything to try and please Kenny, cooking his favorite meals, cutting out clever cartoons from the newspaper that she thought might make him laugh, surprising him with little gifts. No one knew what to do. Then suddenly things seemed better. Kenny came home smiling one afternoon, handing his mother a packet of brochures from Tulane, informing her that he had just enrolled in some graduate courses and was finally going to complete his PhD. Thelma was overjoyed, until a few weeks later when someone from her garden club asked her about the incident at Tulane. Thelma had no idea what the woman was talking about. Apparently, her daughter was in the same graduate program as Kenny, and he had stood up in the middle of class one day and started ranting about some vile plot against him.

Thelma pretended she knew all about it and replied that her son had taken a headache medication that morning that had disagreed with him, and she had given his doctor holy hell about it. The woman from the garden club started to say something, then, thinking better of it, simply thanked Thelma for the tea and left. When Kenny got home later that day, his mother was waiting for him by the door. He knew that look and he was in no mood.

"When were you going to tell me?"

"Tell you what?"

"About your making a fool of yourself at Tulane."

"I did no such thing."

"Kenny, you need help."

"Can we please talk about something else?"

"No, we cannot talk about something else! I may not be able to stop you from embarrassing yourself, but I will not have you continue to humiliate me!"

"That's some talk coming from the person who's been an embarrassment to me my whole life."

Thelma stiffened.

"Do you think I liked my friends being forced to listen to your god-awful piano playing and those stupid songs?"

"Your friends always loved it when I entertained. I distinctly remember them begging to come over all the time."

"You're the one who needs help. Are we done here?"

There was so much Thelma wanted to say. Instead she walked out of the room to tend to her husband.

Kenny's students recognized a dramatic change in their professor. Though he'd never been trim, his belly now protruded over his belt and when his shirt would come untucked, he'd just leave it that way. His face looked pudgy. His perfectly combed hair was oily and unkempt, as if he no longer washed it. His shoes that he had polished regularly were in need of repair. When one of his students would ask a question, his answer would be tinged with sarcasm. If anyone requested extra help, their normally affable and accommodating teacher would suggest that perhaps they weren't cut out for college and might want to consider beauty school. By Christmas, the administration at Dominican had received numerous complaints about Professor Toole. As a Catholic institution that prided itself on tolerance and compassion, the administration sat Kenny down and informed him that he needed to do some serious soul-searching over the holidays, that if they could help him in any way, to please let them know, but if things didn't improve they'd have to let him go.

The first day of the new semester Kenny had coffee and breakfast with his mother. She had arisen extra early that morning and picked up a box of fresh beignets from his favorite bakery. Kenny devoured three, spilling powdered sugar on his tie. Thelma watched him attempt to brush off the sugar with his hands, smearing it deeper into the fabric. She prayed he would go back to his bedroom and change his tie. He got up from the table, put on his coat, thanked her for the beignets, and walked outside.

That evening when Kenny returned home, his mother was in the living room waiting for him. She had been there for hours, trying to figure out what she was going to say to the son she loved so dearly. Thelma had drawn the curtains and was sitting in the dark. Though she had wrapped a blanket around her shoulders, she felt chilled. The phone call she'd received after Kenny left that morning had hollowed her. She pressed her hands against her stomach, remembering when she had been pregnant, the heat inside her womb as her precious child grew within her. She remembered the first time she saw his face, and how bright and alert he was, taking in everything that surrounded him. She had read somewhere that some babies are born old souls and carry the wisdom of a thousand lifetimes in their eyes. She knew her Kenny would suffer, that children burdened with that special light always did. As she cradled her beloved newborn, she vowed that she would protect him from cruelty and injustice, that she would never allow anyone to hurt him. Today she came to accept the awful truth that no mother can protect a child from himself.

Regret washed over her as the images pounded her in waves, her little boy dressed in his costume ready for his performance in her Christmas pageant, looking miserable, but she pushed him the way she always pushed him, and now she wished she could take it all back, let him play with his friends and get grass stains on his good pants and roll in the mud, and climb trees, and not worry about whether he'd fall and hurt himself, because today he did fall and he did hurt himself and now he was hurting her and their family, and maybe if she'd allowed him to fall from trees, he would know how to get back up, because she didn't know how to make him upright again, and it was her fault, her fault, her fault.

"Mom, you're shivering."

"Where did you go today, Kenny?"

"Nowhere, I was teaching."

"The head of the English department called. He asked for you. When I told him you weren't here, he wanted to know where he might find you, because a room full of students had been waiting since 8:00 A.M."

"I got halfway to the college and couldn't keep going."

"That was a good job! How could you be so irresponsible?"

There it was, that tone his mother always had whenever he disappointed her. He had lived his life dutifully, doing what he was told when he was told. He'd honored his father and mother, hadn't taken the Lord's name in vain—well maybe a few times—hadn't coveted his neighbor's wife or bore false witness against him, hadn't worshipped any phony gods, hadn't committed adultery or killed anyone. He hadn't done anything worthy of bringing on this hell that had become his life.

"You have to call the college tomorrow and make things right! Tell them you had an emergency and that you're sorry, that this will never happen again."

Kenny had no intention of calling anyone.

"Kenny, please," Thelma pleaded.

Kenny stood there looking at his mother, shaking and frail, feeling nothing.

"Where are you going?"

Kenny wasn't listening anymore.

ELEVEN

H e woke up disoriented in his car somewhere on Canal Street. Had he slept there all night? He wasn't certain. His last recollection before he passed out was stumbling into an alley and ridding himself of the package containing his manuscript from Simon & Schuster, postmarked third class, which had been sitting in the back seat of his car unopened. He threw it into a large dumpster behind a bar whose name he couldn't conjure.

The night was returning to Kenny in snippets. He remembered his mother trembling and wondering to himself, when had she become so frail? He couldn't stop thinking about her skin, how shriveled her cheeks appeared, and how the talcum powder that she'd always applied so expertly had caked on her chin. He couldn't breathe in that house any longer, and so he'd left. He hadn't wanted to hurt her, not really, but he couldn't control the rage that had been building inside him. It was as if all the years of living someone else's version of himself had ended and he, the real John Kennedy Toole, had finally emerged.

It was messy to be sure, and he hadn't intended to disappear without a by-your-leave, but the need to escape had consumed him and he knew if he didn't go, he would cease to exist. John Kennedy Toole was determined he would not be forgotten, and that Ignatius, whom he'd put in that god-awful box in his closet, would finally be released and light up the sky; and for this reason, and others he had yet to understand but soon would, he erased himself from that house and that woman and that life and that lie, and so he slammed the door and the sound was like music to his withered spirit, and he let the rush of the cold winter air fill his lungs and nourish his resolve.

Methodically, he began his morning. First he went to the bank. When he directed the teller to withdraw his entire savings, she hesitated. A pretty girl, not more than twenty years old, she asked him if he was going on a vacation, to which he answered yes. She wanted to inquire where he was headed, but he didn't seem talkative. As the teller watched him leave, something about the way he walked, how each step was measured, reminded her of the boys from ROTC in high school; they walked the same way, determined but vacant. Usually when customers came in to withdraw funds for a vacation, they were happy and excited.

Next stop, clothes. This would be tricky, John thought. He didn't want another confrontation with his mother. He parked the car in front of the apartment, closed his eyes, and summoned the coldhearted part of himself that he wasn't proud of but knew was there, the part that allowed him to mimic others even when he realized it hurt them, that laughed at the misfortune of strangers and used it for literary fodder. Then he envisioned his parents. Attachments cannot be counted on, he thought, and he remembered the line from Sophocles: "Love is like the ice held in the hand by children."

To his surprise, the house was quiet. What Kenny didn't know was that his mother was upstairs asleep. She had been up all night and when she finally did fall asleep, it was the deep slumber that resembles a small death.

Kenny went to his bedroom, and the boy who had always been a fastidious packer, folding each item just so, threw clothes into his suitcase and stuffed it shut. Next, he took a box down from his closet, grabbed the smaller of two manuscripts that were inside, and put it in his briefcase along with a few of his favorite composition books and his lucky pen. As he was making sure he hadn't forgotten anything, he could hear the creaking of the floor beneath his feet, the hiss of the furnace down the hall, the flushing of a toilet, a telephone ringing, and he committed these sounds to memory, for they were the innocuous music to which his family moved, without knowing it was playing just for them.

J. D. Toole saw his son leaving with a suitcase and valise. Kenny must be going on a trip, he thought, and went to the kitchen to get him an apple. By the time he returned, Kenny was in the car. J.D. went outside and called to his son from the front steps. It was cold and the old man was shivering. Kenny tightened his hands on the steering wheel and drove away.

"Where are we going?" Ignatius asked.

Kenny turned on the radio. It was rush hour and traffic was heavy. While he was stopped at a red light, the person in the car next to him kept staring at the driver arguing with an empty passenger seat.

"How dare you ignore me! Have you no moral decency!" Ignatius shouted.

"No sir, I do not have any moral decency, nor any other kind of decency at this moment. Now if you would be so kind as to let me drive in peace."

Ignatius remained quiet the rest of the day. By nightfall he was growing agitated again and decided to try a different tack. "If you do not tell me where we are going, I shall summon the authorities who will consider your egregious transgressions crimes of a serious nature."

Kenny felt his temples begin to throb. "Ignatius, please, I don't know where we're going. We're heading west, maybe to Hollywood."

Ignatius licked his lips. "We must find the home of Annette Funicello."

"Perhaps there's a tour that passes by her home," Kenny suggested. "In Hollywood, all the big movie stars live in the same neighborhood, Beverly Hills, and there are buses that take you there."

"I do hope Ms. Funicello doesn't serve us any vegetables."

"Ignatius, I don't know Annette Funicello."

"She will have undoubtedly heard of my exploits."

Kenny sighed and kept driving. When he heard snoring from the back seat, he said a silent prayer of thanks.

The year is 1969. It is the week of January 20. Richard Nixon is inaugurated president of the United States. Gas is thirty-five cents a gallon and young people are wearing bell-bottom jeans and tie-dyed shirts. In the coming weeks, California will be declared a disaster area due to flooding and mudslides. The last edition of the *Saturday Evening Post* will be published and the Boeing 747 will make its first commercial flight.

The Rand McNally road map that Kenny had picked up at a gas station a hundred miles back sat in the passenger seat untouched, still wrapped in its plastic sheath. Kenny didn't want maps or routes. He hungered for release, to drive where he wanted when he wanted, explore little dirt roads, stop at diners and eat whatever the hell he felt like, drink until he was satiated, behave however he wished without being judged. This was not a road trip. It was a sojourn into the unknown. As Kenny drove, he paid little attention to the trail he was on or the long stretches of highway that went on forever like ribbon candy, cool and smooth, unfurling before him as far as he could see.

Kenny began to laugh. His eyes were watering and he was coughing. Ignatius felt a surge of compassion for his creator. Clearly the man was sick. Ignatius believed that the burden of their immortality would soon rest upon his shoulders alone, that their fate was contingent upon his fortitude. He would persevere and ensure that their story would be shared and read forever.

The creator had grown quiet and was stopping at a motel. The place looked dilapidated and seedy, probably owned by communists, Ignatius thought. He imagined cockroaches fitted with tiny cameras scurrying around the rooms, recording the comings and goings of guests, and relaying the footage to the bosses drinking vodka in glass-plated offices, discussing who to recruit. Ignatius determined that he must call his nemesis Myrna Minkoff and warn her, but first he had to tuck his creator into bed and make sure he got a good night's sleep. He had heard somewhere that sleep can stave off disorders of the mind.

Thelma would have been disgusted by this motel. Old and neglected, it smelled faintly of urine. Kenny could see his mama now, out of breath, chest heaving, frantically trying to escape, leaving a cloud of talcum powder in her wake. Yes, Kenny said to himself, Thelma would hate this place, and he smiled as he pulled a crisp, new ten-dollar bill out of his pocket to pay for the night's accommodations.

Ignatius was livid but trying to maintain his dignity. How dare I be subjected to this hovel, he said to himself. The gods were cruel indeed, but he would not allow these temporary circumstances to thwart his mission. He was to be the keeper of the flame.

Before Kenny went to sleep, he was preparing to write an important letter. At first, he didn't want to use his lucky pen for this writing task because it hadn't been that lucky. On the other hand, his favorite uncle had given him that pen as a gift and it was high time, Kenny concluded, that its ink be used for greatness instead of failure. He had been pondering this correspondence for a long time. After all, it was arguably the most important thing he would ever write. Should it go to his parents, or should he write several letters, one for each of the important people in his life? No, he thought, that's a terrible idea. I'd have to write a letter to everyone I know because they all think they're important. Kenny stretched his arms above his head and leaned back in thinking position. The bed squeaked in protest and he wondered if it might break and he'd fall through the floor, into the lobby, crushing someone. He imagined the surprised looks on everyone's faces when a portly writer in flannel pajamas came crashing through the ceiling.

Kenny was doing what all good writers do when they're afraid of the blank page. He was allowing his mind to wander, hoping it would find its own way. It was crazy, he thought, to be struggling with a letter. He'd written hundreds of them.

The next morning Ignatius wanted to sleep in, but his creator was having none of it. "Time to experience this great country of ours!" Kenny shouted. Ignatius followed Kenny out to the car, grumbling.

As the days turned into weeks, they drove from dawn to dusk, stopping at motels at night, and then repeating. Every place seemed the same to Ignatius. Though he'd never seen buffalo or antelope roam before, once he'd been exposed to the creatures, he determined they weren't as majestic as he'd hoped. Kenny was enjoying himself, absorbing every detail. Some afternoons it was mile after mile of cattle ranches or dairy farms. Other days, Kenny would find himself driving through hundreds of miles of open land thick with evergreens. To strangers he was just another tourist passing through town, someone they could sell a keychain to or some other cheap bauble, reminding him that he'd been there. While they were making their way through the Colorado Rockies, Ignatius prayed to Fortuna for their safe delivery. There were signs everywhere warning motorists of falling rocks. Ignatius didn't like it and he, unlike his creator, had his priorities straight. He was also tired of roadside food. The only redeeming element of this trip so far was Texas. Ignatius discovered he had a fondness for barbecued ribs. He could devour a slab and a half, secretly wishing there was more.

Kenny was surprised that Ignatius had lasted this long. He was expecting his protagonist to carry on and complain and try to persuade him to return home to New Orleans. Perhaps Kenny had underestimated him.

Ignatius was evolving.

But Kenny had left all that behind. He still hadn't finished the letter. He'd start and then stop, ripping out page after page of his composition book. He'd left a trail of crumpled note paper across five states and he was still no closer to getting it right than he had been two weeks earlier.

Ignatius wanted this letter to be in Kenny's own words, but he was beginning to worry that he may have to write it for him. Ignatius had been discussing the situation with his mother, Irene Reilly, and his savior, Myrna Minkoff, the two most important women in his life, and they agreed that Ignatius must continue holding up their creator. They knew he wasn't right. Perhaps it was the way he looked at himself in the mirror, as if he didn't recognize the man staring back at him, or the half-light in his eyes he tried to hide. There was no denying that John Kennedy Toole was receding, no longer wanting to occupy his own soul. It was the inevitable and noble choice, Kenny thought, so why not abandon decorum, fuck the social graces his mother insisted upon, and gorge on moments, forgetting the whole, existing only on the bounties of the here and now? Fulfilling the desires of the dying was a fraught ritual. Kenny's face was breaking out and his lips were chapped. His mouth breathed a rare flower most people made a point to avoid.

Kenny's heart was set on reaching California. He'd dreamed about visiting Hollywood since he was a boy. He'd followed his favorite movie stars and was encouraged by how much he had in common with them. They started out as nobodies, too. Judy Garland was a sweet unassuming girl from the Midwest named Frances Gumm. Kenny thought of himself and Judy as kindred spirits. They both had determined mothers, and Kenny often wondered, if it wasn't for Mrs. Gumm's relentlessness, would Judy still just be Frances, another pretty thing with a voice like an angel who worked as a waitress or taught Sunday school, dreaming of a different life? Cary Grant, whom Kenny considered the handsomest leading man in film, was born in England with the unfortunate name of Archibald Leach, and his parents worked in a clothing factory, yet he became a star. Kenny knew the stories of all his favorite stars. Clark Gable, Fred Astaire, Joan Crawford, Bette Davis, Rita Hayworth, Jean Harlow, and of course his beloved Marilyn were mythical figures, like the gods of ancient Greece, fallible and human yet transcendent. Death didn't kill movie stars; it kept them alive. Kenny wanted some of that, and he also had an obligation to Ignatius. Ignatius was all he had now, the only thing between himself and obscurity. Ignatius deserved the spotlight. As Kenny wound his way across the country, something was forcing him to continue, to not stop until he'd reached his destination. He knew that once he did, everything would be all right and so he drove and drove, singing a happy tune.

The Pacific Coast Highway welcomed John Kennedy Toole. He had all the windows open so that the cool ocean breeze reinvigorated his senses. He wanted to taste the sea spray and stuck his tongue out playfully like a child trying to capture snowflakes. He could hear the roar of the surf and imagined the people living in these beach towns. He wanted to walk among them unnoticed, to blend into their routine and become one with this place and the waves and the water, the infinite blues and grays, the unpredictability of nature, right there, life, beating, breathing, in the rhythmic movement of the tides. This was Eden and Kenny wanted to enjoy the garden before biting into the apple. He stopped at the small towns dotting the coast. He ate fish so succulent and delicious that he ordered two, sometimes three helpings. He also tried an avocado for the first time. A boy was selling them for a dollar a bushel on the side of the road. Kenny decided he'd never tasted anything as curiously satisfying before. The boy showed him how to make guacamole and mixed Kenny a small tub of the spicy dip for the drive, along with a bag of homemade tortilla chips. He was thriving here as he knew that he would. There was sand everywhere, in the car, in the bed, in his shoes.

It was on this part of the trip, between San Diego and Dana Point, that John Kennedy Toole finally was able to write the letter. It was a moment familiar to any writer, when suddenly the words you'd been struggling to find avail themselves. He could hear them inside his head. Kenny was sipping a glass of white wine at a seaside joint, gazing at the ocean, when it happened. He had been hoping it would be like this. He assembled his lucky pen, his notebook, and released the captured bird of his thoughts, filling one page after another, unburdening himself.

Tears stung Kenny's eyes. Trying to explain to his dad what he was planning was near impossible. He would never understand. Thelma, on the other hand, might, though he doubted she'd ever admit it. She admired fame and believed she had been cheated of it. Kenny would fix that. It would mean more to her than grandchildren, a gift he wished he could give her, but this was a sacrifice he was willing to make for them both. He wrote until he was spent, and then he wrote again a few hours later, and again after that, until the sentences stretched out like the path he had been traveling.

By the time Kenny reached Los Angeles, he wanted to explore the land of his boyhood fantasies. He consulted the map of Hollywood attractions that he'd bought at a previous motel along with a bottle of Coke and a package of gum drops.

First stop, Grauman's Chinese Theater, where celebrities left hand- and footprints in the cement. He purchased a ticket from the visitors' booth and asked where he might find Marilyn. The clerk, without looking up, handed Kenny a guide map, saying everyone was listed alphabetically. It took only minutes for Kenny to locate her. Two adjacent concrete blocks both signed on the same date, June 26, 1953. One autograph was Marilyn's and the other Jane Russell's. They had scrawled the words first on one block and finished it on the next: GENTLEMEN PREFER BLONDES. Kenny admired the raven-haired Russell's sense of humor. Then he kneeled down and carefully placed his palms over Marilyn's, closing his eyes, imagining that they were dancing in a courtyard, laughing and twirling, joined forever in spirit. He would have stayed that way, absorbing her through the rough concrete, had a security guard not interrupted him.

Kenny spent two days in Hollywood. He went on a bus tour of Beverly Hills, visited the La Brea Tar Pits and Paramount Studios, had lunch at the Farmers Market, drove out to Knott's Berry Farm, and spent an evening at the Troubadour. The performer that night reminded him of Joan, the girl he'd met in Greenwich Village at the Gaslight almost a decade earlier. He heard her on the radio sometimes, and he wondered what might have happened if he'd accepted her invitation to meet her friends. Kenny regretted that decision. There was so much he should have done differently.

Kenny's next magical destination: Hearst Castle. Kenny had always been fascinated by the story of newspaper magnate William Randolph Hearst and the grand soirees he hosted at "the ranch." The castle, sometimes referred to as San Simeon, was part of a ninety-thousand-square-foot estate that boasted lavish guest houses, a movie theater, a gold indoor pool, art, and a private zoo. Kenny imagined the famous people who'd stayed there: Winston Churchill, Franklin Roosevelt, Charles Lindbergh, Greta Garbo . . . Though Kenny wasn't certain about ghosts, if they did exist he hoped there would be a few famous ones floating around San Simeon. Kenny wanted to stand inside the castle's towering halls and pretend he was someone important like those who'd been there before him. He longed to breathe the same air they breathed and let that power and influence soak into his skin. John Kennedy Toole had not been invited there but he could pretend that he would have belonged, and this trip was all pretend anyway because it would end as it had begun, with the closing of a door and the turning of a key. Kenny didn't want to think about that now. He had purchased a ticket for the tour and heard the guide asking everyone in their group to gather by the main entrance. He slipped the ticket stub into his pocket and joined the others.

Later that day, Kenny pondered whether he was making the right decision. Parents sacrificed for their children all the time, he thought. Besides, he'd lived a full life, all things considered. This trip was what he needed and he must not waver. When Ignatius asked Kenny where they would be staying that night, he was told, "Under the stars." Ignatius was not amused.

"Ignatius, we're running low on money. I can't afford a motel every night. We need what's left to get back to Biloxi."

Ignatius considered this. If they didn't return to Biloxi, it would ruin everything. He reluctantly took the blanket his creator was handing him, spread it on the ground, and laid down. Within minutes he was asleep. Kenny retrieved his valise from the car and pulled out the one manuscript he'd brought. Just a handful of pages. He remembered those hours locked away in his room, angrily pounding the typewriter keys. He and Ellen had spoken by phone earlier that day so many months ago, and though it wasn't anything that either one had said, they both sensed an elemental change had taken place. It wasn't long after that they would see each other for the last time. Kenny felt a familiar ache whenever he thought of her. If he ever married, she would be the one. But he realized that would be selfish and unfair. He remembered the concern and anticipation in her expression when he met her at the airport. Kenny knew that if he told her, she would find a way to stop him, and he couldn't let her do that. So he'd treated her cruelly, pushed her away, forced her to feel such disgust that she would never be tempted to return. When she left, he wept for everything he would never know. Yes, there were times when he could convince himself he didn't want any of that, but then, a yearning would grow again, and he'd struggle not to feel it. He'd drink, he'd fight with Thelma and write short stories like the one he was holding in his hands but that part of him couldn't bear. Kenny didn't have a flashlight so he turned the motor on, sat in the cool grass, and read in the glow of the headlights.

He'd titled the story "Disillusionment." He'd considered changing it but liked the way the word sounded. Perhaps it was the perfect title. As he read the story again, making occasional edits, he realized just how distraught he must have been when he wrote it. The characters were scattered, and the narrative was confusing, jumping between time periods without any links. Not his best work to be sure, he thought. Like *The Neon Bible*, it too was a dark and depressing tale. That's why he loved Ignatius and everyone living in *Dunces*. They made him laugh. And he knew they'd make others laugh, too. Not like that *Superworm* book, Kenny said to himself. Kenny turned the headlights off and laid down. Tomorrow they would turn around and head back to Georgia, the second to last stop of their adventure.

March 2004. Bill Greeley was sitting on a bench at Tulane University in uptown New Orleans. Before he left, he'd gotten a call from his contact at the *New York Post*, who said they were no longer interested in his article, that it came from the top and there was nothing he could do. Greeley wondered if his sniffing around had had anything to do with it, and like any good journalist, it fueled his determination. He telephoned the entertainment editor at the competing *New York Daily News*. She and Greeley knew each other from many late nights at P.J. Clarke's. A smart, no-nonsense newswoman who'd started out as a college intern, she was immediately intrigued by the idea of a backstory on *A Confederacy of Dunces* and okayed the piece. His deadline was the end of the week. He had been in New Orleans for days, immersed in research, and was requesting more time.

"I've stumbled onto something that I think could be major, but need time to follow it through."

When she asked him what he'd found, all he said was that a lot of smart people may have gotten it wrong. The excitement in his voice was persuasive.

"How much time are we talking here?"

"Just one more week and I'll file."

Trusting Bill's instincts, she agreed to extend the deadline.

Greeley was frustrated by the paucity of primary source material on Toole. He had asked Professor Bell to talk to Gottlieb, since they knew each other socially, and though the renowned editor was polite, he wasn't forthcoming. Greeley wondered if the man had learned of Kenny's suicide somehow when it happened, or if he found out years later when the book was published. He imagined it must have saddened him.

Greeley was relentless. When one avenue didn't pan out, he'd resolve himself to uncovering the next. He had already spent nearly a week exploring the French Quarter, visiting all the places Kenny frequented that were still there, the Old Absinthe being the most interesting. He understood its allure. It had a quality to it that made you want to drink excessively, which Greeley did, and then regretted the next morning. He'd hired a guide to drive him to the homes where Kenny grew up. One of them, the apartment on Cambronne Street, was for sale, and to Greeley's surprise the front door was open, so he just walked in. He recalled his conversation with Kenny's old friend from Southern Louisiana Institute, Joel, and tried to imagine the Tooles on a typical day, Kenny's father wandering about the house, testing the doorknobs, or his mother making notes in the dining room for her next pageant. The place had clearly been unoccupied for a while. Greeley had done his due diligence and still wasn't satisfied. Kenny's death certificate and police report were destroyed in a fire, and the few people who knew Kenny had little to offer. Some couldn't remember details; others felt uncomfortable talking about the dead. Joel had been the most helpful, but he admitted that he couldn't shed more light on Kenny's final days than Greeley had already uncovered in the archives at Tulane.

Greeley was interested in the last leg of the trip, especially his visit to Flannery O'Connor's home in Georgia and his time in Biloxi. Greeley had a theory about great writers and artists, that they perceived death differently than other people, that for them the afterlife wasn't about the hope of heaven, but rather the promise of their work. Kenny would want that, too. How far would he have gone to achieve it? Kenny was so full of life. He lived in one of the most colorful cities in the world and had captured its magic in a way that no other writer had before or since. Greeley had read everything he could get about Toole. Most of it concluded that Kenny succumbed to mental illness and killed himself out of despair. Greeley didn't believe it; perhaps it was because it was a cliché and Kenny's gift to the world deserved a braver understanding of what happened. He realized he was inviting criticism but Kenny's story was worth it. He felt for the guy because he'd been there. When he continued to receive rejection after rejection for his novel, and the old man kept pushing him to get a proper job and stop pursuing such nonsense, he remembered going to the bank and putting his manuscript in his safe-deposit box, along with a note. He had the whole thing figured out. He would kill himself that night, pills, and leave the key to the deposit box next to his pillow. He imagined how the story would be reported by the media, which he would have laid out for them in the suicide note, and the look on the old man's face when he read it and his mother's regret. This book was his baby, and he'd made the sacrifice that would let it live on. And if the writing was there, and he wanted to believe that it was, so much so that he was willing to die for it to be read, then the book would go on forever. He wondered if Kenny had the same fear. That was what moved Greeley. Kenny knew his writing was good and that's why he went through with his plan. Greeley didn't, and that's why after swallowing only four Valiums, he stuck his finger down his throat.

Greeley didn't call Professor Bell to discuss his theory. He needed more evidence, so he made copies of the last few items from the archives, rented a car, and headed toward Biloxi. He knew that Kenny had died somewhere off Popps Ferry Road. He'd consulted contemporary maps but they offered little clarification. There had been so much construction in the area over the years, he feared he wouldn't be able to find anyone who might recall the writer who was found dead in the woods in a blue Chevy Chevelle. As he crossed into Biloxi, he noticed a landmark building with a sign out front that read BILOXI HISTORICAL SOCIETY and a phone number. He dialed the number. A young woman answered. He explained why he was in town and she told him that a lot of the families that lived out that way had been there for generations. She gave him directions and said if she thought of anything else, she'd call.

As he was turning off the main road, he saw a lawnmower parts and repair shop, the kind that were vanishing across America, with a sign that had probably been there since the 1930s, and a selection of rusty lawnmowers sitting out back. Greeley loved places like this, untouched by the modern world. He parked and went inside. When he opened the door, an old-fashioned bell signaled his arrival. A man whom Greeley judged to be in his early sixties, with a long beard, wearing bib overalls, greeted him warmly and asked how he could help. Greeley explained why he was in town.

"You don't happen to know of any old-timers around here that might remember the incident?" Greeley asked.

The man showed him to the back office, where he introduced him to his dad, Al. Greeley reached out and shook the old man's hand. He had to be well into his eighties, but his grip was firm and his eyes were alert and the deepest blue Greeley had ever seen. He was dressed in overalls like his son, and was sporting a cap proclaiming the name of the shop. He had a deep Southern accent and his voice was warm and engaging. Al knew about John Kennedy Toole. The day they found him, Al's youngest grandchild was born, and he remembered the folks at the hospital talking about the accident. When *A*

Confederacy of Dunces came out years later, like a lot of people in Biloxi, he bought it and he read it.

"Shame about that poor fellow," Al said. "He was a damn good writer. I've never been much of a reader, but that one was worth my time."

"I'd like to find the spot where he died."

"If you follow Popps Ferry for just under two miles, there's a dirt road on the right that'll take you through the backwoods. It's on this side of the causeway. Keep following it until it dead ends. They found him near there."

Greeley took notes. The two men shook hands, then Greeley thanked him for his kindness, and left eager to find the location Al had described before nightfall. As he wound his way through dense woods, he could see the calm, serene waters of the causeway glistening in the distance. When the road ended, he parked and got out. There was a tangled beauty about the place, the way the sun peeked through the trees casting eerie shadows, and how the dark green leaves seemed to be whispering their secrets. He stood there for a long time, just listening, and then reached into his backpack and pulled out one of the documents he'd gotten from the library earlier that day. "Okay, Kenny, talk to me." Then he sat under one of the giant oaks and began to read.

By the time he'd finished "Disillusionment," the moon was out and the sounds of katydids pierced the lonely silence. Greeley could almost feel Kenny there beside him. Greeley remained still and absorbed the images taking shape in his mind, unfolding like bits of film, each one blending into the next, revealing a long-awaited truth. In that extraordinary moment, Greeley let go of doubt, just as Kenny's spirit had done thirty-five years earlier under the same majestic oak. Greeley would look back on this experience and remember every detail, convinced something really did happen that night that he would never be able to fully explain.

TWELVE

⁂

T he weather is cloudy and warm in the Big Easy with temperatures dropping into the low fifties overnight and rain likely tomorrow. Location: a funeral home in a working-class section of New Orleans.

The service was solemn. Kenny's immediate family and his babysitter from childhood were the only people in attendance. Ignatius now regretted the plan. How could he have agreed to something so preposterous? Why hadn't he thought things through more carefully? How would he escape the box in the closet now? Ashes to ashes. Dust to dust. In *God* we trust? Ignatius reeled with the unfairness of it all. In that moment, watching his creator's father staring at the coffin as if waiting for his son to wake up, Ignatius Reilly wept.

It is Friday, March 28, 1969. President Dwight D. Eisenhower has just died at the age of seventy-eight. Newlyweds John Lennon and Yoko Ono are in the midst of staging their first "Bed-In for Peace" at the Amsterdam Hilton. A month later, Charles de Gaulle will resign as president of France, and Richard Nixon will award Duke Ellington the Presidential Medal of Freedom.

In New York City, at Rockefeller Center, in the offices of Simon & Schuster, it was the beginning of another busy day. Editors were reading manuscripts, negotiating acquisitions, making decisions about which titles would command the house's frontlist that coming fall. Production assistants were circulating approvals on cover designs. A mail clerk was delivering the morning's interoffice memos. A slush pile of manuscripts lined the walls of the editorial department, most of which would never be read. An overworked assistant would eventually return each one third-class with a form letter, never imagining that among them might be a Great American Novel left to languish in its scuffed envelope. The hopeful writers who submitted these manuscripts without benefit of a literary agent would find their precious work back on their doorstep, the pages as crisp as they were when it was sent, a signal that no one had even opened it. The big New York houses rarely thought about the destinies of these slush pile writers.

April is the cruelest month. Back on Hampson Street in New Orleans, Thelma toiled over a pot of gumbo. She measured out each ingredient, meticulously following the recipe in her *Better Homes and Gardens* cookbook that Kenny had given her for her birthday the previous year. She had been disappointed when she opened his present, annoyed that her son, who'd been watching her make delicious meals his whole life and had never once seen her use a recipe, had suddenly decided she required such assistance. Since when did she have to consult recipes? She could have published her own cookbook once upon a time.

"Doesn't it smell wonderful, Kenny? I bought the crawfish fresh this morning just like the book suggested and I had the butcher prepare the sausage special for us. Have I told you how much I adore your birthday present, my darling boy? Such a thoughtful gift."

If anyone had overheard, they would have believed Kenny was sitting at the table, awaiting his steaming bowl of gumbo. It was precisely why Arthur, who was in the dining room reviewing some papers for his sister, was growing more concerned. It was unnerving enough that his brother-in-law still wandered into Kenny's room some nights to tuck him in. It was like something from the theater of the absurd. J.D.'s confusion had almost become a comfort to Thelma because, during those moments, she would pretend that her husband really was putting their son to bed, and she'd become so skilled at this sad game, she swore she could hear her sweet child's eager voice, begging his dad to tell him a bedtime story.

"Kenny, remember the first time you saw me making gumbo? You couldn't have been more than three years old, and you kept asking why I was putting giant bugs in our soup!" Thelma recalled. "You refused to taste it, so I had to make you a grilled cheese instead for dinner. When did you finally start eating gumbo? Wasn't it when you were living in New York?"

"Thelma, he can't hear you," said Arthur from the doorway.

She ignored him, adding exactly one more teaspoon of oregano and a half-teaspoon of garlic salt to her gumbo, stirring gingerly, as if she might interrupt something magical happening inside the pot if she engaged the spoon too vigorously. This was not the Thelma Toole that Arthur knew. That woman never did anything gingerly. She commanded whatever she was cooking the same way she commanded people. It was one of the qualities he'd always admired/abhorred about his sister, how she never considered that someone might not bend to her will or that the soufflé wouldn't rise. Just like she never considered her only child would asphyxiate himself rather than spend another moment with any of them. Arthur was struggling with Kenny's death, but Thelma's pain didn't leave room for anyone else's.

Thelma tasted the gumbo. Satisfied, she put the lid over the pot and removed her apron.

"Thelma, this has to stop."

"What has to stop, Arthur?"

"Thelma, you barely leave the house. And when is the last time you washed your hair or changed your housedress?"

"Worry about yourself, Arthur. You've always been good at that."

"I think you should see someone."

"A psychiatrist? I will not bring more shame upon this house, nor do I have any intention of discussing my private matters with a stranger."

"Then talk to me. You can't just go on talking to your dead son and shutting everyone else out. You're not the only one who's hurting here. Don't you think I miss him, too? I kick myself every day for not recognizing the dark place he was in, for not doing something, anything! I loved him too, Thelma."

"You can angle all you want, Arthur, but I already told you, there was no note."

"This isn't about that."

"Don't you think I would tell you?"

Arthur knew his nephew. Kenny would never leave without saying goodbye.

"Thelma, please."

"Why don't you have some gumbo? I also have some fresh beignets from the bakery, Kenny's favorite."

That night, after Arthur had gone home and her husband was in bed, Thelma lit a fire. She pulled her sewing box out of the linen closet, removed the Big Chief notebook she had placed inside, and tossed it into the fireplace. She watched the flames consume her son's dying words, then turn into embers, barely illuminating the darkness where she remained, beneath the ghostly shadows dancing upon the ceiling. She remembered the afternoon she emptied the original contents of her sewing box, the brightly colored spools of thread, the ornate buttons and bows, the swatches of fabric for holiday costumes and Christmas pageants that she had collected over the years. It was one month earlier, the day that the package from the Biloxi police arrived. She had been expecting it. The envelope came registered mail and, as she was signing for it, she felt relieved that her brother wasn't there. Arthur had been coming around a lot lately, and though he meant well, his visits were growing tiresome. J.D. thought the knock on the door was the Girl Scouts delivering cookies. Thelma, not wanting to explain what had actually been delivered, went into the kitchen, handed him a MoonPie, and told him the Girl Scouts were selling these now. J.D. accepted the sweet treat and the explanation without issue. While he enjoyed his dessert, Thelma dumped everything from her sewing box into a wastepaper bag and left it for the garbageman to pick up the next morning.

She briefly considered donating all those wonderful spools of thread to her church, where they might have been used to fix coats for the homeless, when her thoughts drifted back to Kenny. Was he cold where he was? Did they have coats in heaven? If he was in heaven (Thelma was a Catholic), because suicide wasn't merely against the law, it was a sin. What if her beloved son was stuck in purgatory? No, she said to herself. He had already served his time in that rough place.

The fire crackled and hissed. She stared at a tiny scrap of paper that curled and glowed. For a moment, she wished she would have finished reading the letter that had been tucked inside his notebook, but after the first few sentences, she could bear no more. It wasn't her Kenny who had written that. It was addressed to her, his dad, and Arthur, but it was as if a stranger had left it for them. No, she thought. It was a bad day when he wrote those words, a very bad day. She wanted all of them to remember Kenny's good days, only the best ones. She took a poker from the mantel and with trembling hands made certain the incineration was complete. The only items of his she kept were his lucky pen and the sad little short story he'd written that still bore his edits in the margins. She returned them to her sewing box.

In New York, Kent Carroll, who had returned from Europe and was working for a weekly magazine, was enjoying a rare accomplishment for someone just starting out. He had convinced an executive at Warner Bros. to hire two young filmmakers that he had written a story about, Mike Wadley and Bob Maurice, to shoot the studio's documentary on the Three Days of Peace and Music that was to take place in Woodstock that summer. The executive had chosen someone else for the job, but Kent convinced him to make the change.

Months later Thelma, who swore she could feel her son's presence everywhere, in the whistling of a tea kettle or the rustling of the trees, was watching a news story about that same concert and the much-anticipated documentary. It was the night of her sixty-eighth birthday, and as she stared at the footage of hundreds of thousands of young people camping out in tents and sleeping under the stars, a raven-haired girl began singing "We Shall Overcome" in a voice so sweet and pure Thelma thought she had never heard anything so beautiful. Alone in her living room, on the eve of her first birthday without her child, the tears finally came. Thelma didn't know of Kenny's long-ago encounter with that same young woman at a dimly lit coffee house in Greenwich Village, nor did she catch the singer's name on television, though in her final moments of life, Thelma would hear that melody playing softly. Thelma awoke the next morning stiff and sore, having fallen asleep on the couch. A pile of condolence cards sat on the side table next to her, unopened. She had wanted to go through them, but any reference to her child only made her angry. She grabbed the stack, wrapped a rubber band around them, and put them in her purse. Then she made her husband some oatmeal and left for the market, throwing the notes in the garbage.

Meanwhile in Greenwich Village, Kent Carroll was attending the New York Film Festival. He'd just written a review on one of the films that was being featured, Marguerite Duras's *Destroy She Said*. The publisher of the book upon which the film was based had asked to meet him. While sharing a drink, the publisher admitted that he didn't understand what the damn thing was about until he read Kent's review.

"Neither did I until I read your book," Carroll said.

Over a laugh and more drinks, Barney Rosset asked Kent how much he made at the magazine.

"One hundred fifty dollars a week."

"I'll pay you four hundred."

Two weeks later, Kent Carroll moved into the Grove Press offices on University Place and assumed the roles of staff writer and editor.

One evening during a friendly dinner at Elaine's with his boss and Haskell Wexler, the cinematographer, Wexler began talking about a film he had recently shot that featured a bunch of teenagers contemplating their last year of high school, filmed mostly at night. Apparently, the story had no interesting political convictions or critical social concerns. Even more egregious, the cinematographer complained, was that he'd done this questionable project for scale, and that the producer justified his meager salary by giving him a couple of points after break-even, but this movie was unlikely to make any money. The only reason he'd agreed to it, he said, was because Francis Ford Coppola asked him to as a favor because he had been a mentor to the director.

The next day Carroll bought the publishing rights to the screenplay. In the summer of 1973, *American Graffiti* opened to audiences that had waited in line for hours. Grove Press would sell over three hundred thousand copies of the screenplay. The film would make over one hundred million dollars and Wexler's points of the gross earnings were said to have paid for a substantial home overlooking the ocean in Santa Monica.

During that same year, back in New Orleans, a grieving mother who had stopped distinguishing between the passing of one day and the beginning of the next tended to her husband. Sometimes Thelma would show him photos of Kenny, hoping to jog his memory. He'd stare at the images and she'd wait for some flicker of recognition. Thelma also attempted a biography of Kenny, but she found it impossible to concentrate. Though her body was growing weak, her resolve to keep her son's memory was steadfast. One night, after she'd put J.D. to bed, she took out a composition book and handwrote the words to Elizabeth Barrett Browning's "Sonnet Forty-Three" as a sacred promise between mother and son. Then, as she had done countless times when Kenny was a boy, she read it out loud, her voice strong and sure in the silence.

The year is 2004. The Boston Red Sox have won the World Series for the first time since 1918. Five million new cases of AIDS are reported worldwide. A new social network called Facebook is launched at Harvard by student Mark Zuckerberg and classmates. Mel Gibson's *The Passion of the Christ* is released.

Greeley was hunched over his manual typewriter, pounding out the notes from his trip down South. He had everything organized and had just completed his observations leading up to Kenny's final moments. He realized he should probably be using his laptop, but something about that wonderful clicking sound, the permanence of paper, the satisfying ritual of sliding over the carriage, was for him like driving a stick shift instead of an automatic. Greeley was heartened by everything he'd gleaned in New Orleans and Biloxi, and he'd done some research in New York that had proven fruitful. There were still unanswered questions, but at least now, he felt confident proceeding. Just as he was about to quit for the night, his phone rang.

"How's the research going?"

Professor Bell's voice was unmistakable. Greeley related what he'd uncovered since their last meeting, after poring through the Toole archives at Tulane and visiting the places where Kenny grew up, how he retraced Kenny's steps before his death, his conversation with the old timer at the lawn mower repair shop, and the insights that Kenny's friend Joel had shared with him. The professor listened patiently, sensing his former student was holding something back, and pressed him.

"You'll think I'm certifiable," Greeley said.

"It is a risk I shall take."

"When I went to the spot where Kenny supposedly died, something happened."

"Go on."

"This is going to sound nutty, but it was getting dark by then, and it was sort of eerie, and all of a sudden I understood why he did what he did that night, as if he were sitting there explaining it to me."

"That doesn't sound so nutty."

⁂

It was 1972, three days after Christmas. Thelma leaned over the casket and removed a piece of lint from her husband's jacket, then patting his hand, she bid her final farewell to the man she'd lived with for nearly a half century. At seventy-one years old, she moved slowly, her steps deliberate. She would stop every so often, straighten her shoulders self-consciously, and then continue walking, her shoes scuffed where she favored one side.

A few months later, she was walking past Kenny's room when something compelled her to turn the knob and step inside. She didn't believe in ghosts or spirits, though on some sleepless nights when she would have given almost anything to have her family back, she wondered if Ouija boards worked.

The room smelled stale. Kenny had left the place a mess. She'd intended to clean it up. The desk that had always been pristine was strewn with wrinkled, half-graded papers and a coffee-stained folder that read English Literature, Professor Toole, sitting beside them. His No. 2 pencils that he sharpened every morning and would line up just so next to his stack of composition books were worn down to the nub and askew. A discarded typewriter ribbon was on the floor. It looked like some stranger had been rummaging through her son's things. Thelma felt a chill and took a sweater out of his closet and wrapped it around her shoulders. It was the first time she had been in his closet since he departed. She chose the bright blue cashmere that she'd gotten him their final Christmas together. She had put it on layaway at D.H. Holmes. It took months before she could finally take it home. It fit her Kenny perfectly. Thelma had promised the local Salvation Army some of her son's items for their annual auction. Steeling herself for this long overdue task, she began going through Kenny's closet. Then she noticed the box.

There wasn't a mark or a smudge on it. He had valued whatever was inside. She placed it on the bed and opened it. The title page read *A Confederacy of Dunces*. Kenny had only let her read bits and pieces before. She turned to the first page and began reading.

The next morning, she woke up still in Kenny's bed, having fallen asleep just before dawn, a stack of pages beside her. She knew that she would not, could not, rest until this was published. In the kitchen, she made herself a hearty breakfast of scrambled eggs and bacon, and with renewed purpose mapped out a plan.

For the next week, each morning at precisely 6:00 A.M., Thelma would wake up, get dressed, and take a bus to the library. It was a long walk from the bus stop, and by the time she reached the front steps, she'd often be out of breath. Thelma didn't know how publishers acquired manuscripts. The father of one of the girls she'd given elocution and music lessons to had authored a book on gumbo and she'd called him late one night for advice. His daughter was married with a baby on the way. It had been years since Thelma had any contact with the family and the man couldn't quite place who this woman was who had called him at such an inappropriate hour, going on about some literary masterpiece and a genius son. He felt sorry for her, and wanting to be helpful, suggested she check *The Literary Marketplace*, an annual publication that listed all the literary agents and publishers in the country, that she might start there.

Thelma would sit at the long wooden table in the resource room, her hat and gloves placed neatly in the adjacent chair, looking up names and addresses of publishers, then meticulously recording them in one of the composition books she'd found on Kenny's desk. Arthur had encouraged her to research literary agents, warning her that submitting to publishers directly would repeat the mistake Kenny made, but the more he tried to convince her, the more she resisted. "No," Thelma thought. "I will not entrust literature of this magnitude to some two-bit pitch man." A kind volunteer at the library wondered what Thelma was doing there every day, noticing that she moved slowly, as if in pain. "I walk in this world for my son," she'd answer.

Thelma wasn't certain which publishers to send the manuscript to, so she chose the ones that had published the books in her own library at home that she'd read to Kenny when he was a child. Next, she consulted her cherished copy of Emily Post's *Etiquette*, determined to adhere to the proper standards of comportment as she navigated the mysteries of publishing.

As Watergate raged on, women's rights advocates celebrated the *Roe v. Wade* ruling, and millions of families tuned into *The Waltons* every Thursday night, a determined old woman living alone on Hampson Street in New Orleans continued the crusade for her only child. One day on her way home from the library, she went to the stationery store and ordered personalized letterhead and envelopes. She winced when the clerk rang up the total, but she could go without for a while. Ignatius, she thought, must have a proper introduction. Next stop, the office supply store. Arthur had told her that they had one of those fancy new Xerox machines in the back and suggested she ask if they could make a copy of the manuscript. Thelma didn't like the idea of sending a copy to anyone. She wanted publishers to have the actual manuscript that her son had held in his hands, and to experience the same sense of awe she'd felt when she'd discovered and read it. It never occurred to her that if she sent the original, it might be lost or that the publisher might not return it. In the genteel world in which this remarkable Southern woman lived, one had manners and Thelma Ducoing Toole imagined that publishers, the purveyors of literature and culture, would not, could not, conceive of losing anything upon which the written word was typed. Thelma didn't know of slush piles and overworked assistants, or of corporations that cared no more about her son's work than they did any unknown novelist's work.

On a chilly afternoon in March 1973, Thelma removed Kenny's lucky pen from her sewing box and handwrote a brief note addressed To Whom It May Concern, kindly requesting the enclosed manuscript be considered for publication. Then she wrapped *A Confederacy of Dunces* in tissue paper, put it in a box, and sent it off to the first publisher on her list, Alfred A. Knopf, unaware that its editor in chief had recently arrived from Simon & Schuster and had already read those very pages, that it was Kenny who had sent the manuscript to him a lifetime ago. Perhaps if she had known, she would have gotten a timelier response.

Each day, before she retrieved the mail, Thelma prayed. As the weeks turned into months, she waited and hoped. Nothing. Thelma started calling and writing letters to Knopf requesting they return the manuscript, that it was her only copy, but she was never able to get beyond the switchboard. She contacted a literary agent entreating upon him to intervene, to no avail. Finally, on a sweltering

July afternoon, the mailman delivered the manuscript back to Hampson Street. It was still in the same box wrapped in the same tissue paper along with a form letter politely rejecting it.

Publisher after publisher, they all declined. Most sent form letters, others typed notes, indicating this just wasn't right for their list. With each agonizing period of waiting followed by yet another disappointment, Thelma's health declined. Artist Pablo Picasso would die; heiress Patty Hearst would be kidnapped; Hank Aaron would score his seven hundred fifteenth home run; an American president would resign and another president, Jimmy Hoffa, would go missing; all as a relentless Thelma Toole was no longer able to make the journey to the post office or write another note. Three years would pass during which *A Confederacy of Dunces* would remain where Thelma had left it, by the door, wrapped in tissue paper, ready for its next submission. There were days when photos of her son were her only company. When the doctor finally convinced Thelma that it would be best if she didn't live alone, she moved in with Arthur. On the day that he picked her up, all she brought were a few suitcases with her clothing and some personal items. He had everything else put in storage.

Under Arthur's care, Thelma would regain her strength, and as America prepared for its bicentennial, Thelma began submitting the manuscript again. Each time she would send the original document, refusing, even after Arthur had copies made, to present anything else. Arthur could never understand it, but he knew when it was best to give in, lest he endure one of her god-awful tirades. And they'd been more frequent as of late. Arthur tried to be patient, but this was not a woman who inspired one's magnanimous impulses. She'd been particularly irritable since she'd heard from a little-known African American publisher that they, too, had no interest in publishing *A Confederacy of Dunces*. Arthur had tried to explain to Thelma that their rejection was understandable given the fact they only published black authors.

Then one day his sister simply went too far. She came into the kitchen, just as he was about to enjoy his morning tea and a soft-boiled egg, and put a chauffeur's jacket and cap in his lap.

"What on earth?"

"Hurry up and get dressed! I've already polished your good shoes. They're by the front door."

"I'm not going anywhere and certainly not dressed like something out of *Masterpiece Theater*."

"You are going to put on that jacket and cap right this minute and drive me to an important appointment."

Walker Percy was just about to leave his office at Loyola University, a lovely campus adjacent to Tulane, when she descended upon him in a cloud of talcum powder. Percy, a quintessential Southern gentleman whose wry sense of humor and quiet, affable demeanor endeared him to his peers and students alike, had been taught to treat ladies with respect.

Thelma Toole was unlike any lady he had ever encountered, with her 1950s hat, rouge-stained cheeks, and white gloves. At first, he thought she was the grandparent of a grad student whom he'd recently recommended for a fellowship.

The student had mentioned to Percy that his grandmother was his biggest fan and not to be surprised if she waltzed into his office with fresh pralines to thank him for helping her grandson. When the famed novelist saw Thelma, he greeted her warmly only to be surprised a second time, when instead of a bag of chewy pralines and a thank-you note, she handed him a manuscript, a very large one, introduced herself as Thelma Ducoing Toole, John Kennedy's Toole's mother, and then proceeded to tell him their story. He realized he would not be getting home as early as planned.

Percy had to admit, Mrs. Toole was articulate and her elocution was the most perfect he'd ever heard. It was as if a character from a Tennessee Williams play were performing a monologue just for him and if he so much as blinked, she would disappear into the ether. He was as transfixed as he was annoyed by this charming woman who was clearly devoted to her child. It was then that Percy learned that her son had taken his own life. He was struck by the matter-of-fact way in which Mrs. Toole told him of her son's suicide. She didn't make excuses nor hide from the word. She said it simply and plainly, and then asked him to be the bearer of her son's legacy, that it mustn't be lost.

Webster's Dictionary felt lighter than the heavy manuscript she'd bestowed upon him, and for a moment he considered everything on his desk, the stack of assignments that awaited his attention, the requests from journalists eager to interview him about his National Book Award for *The Moviegoer*. This was not a good time to help anyone, not even the powerful likes of a Thelma Toole. He thanked her for the manuscript, promising to read it as soon as he could, then he bid the aging belle and her apparent chauffeur goodbye. He felt for her. Percy's father and grandfather had taken their own lives, and many believed his mother's car accident was also a suicide. Walker Percy knew the blight upon the soul that the suicide of a loved one created, and for a mother to lose a child that way had to have been the most blinding of all pain. Percy didn't hold out much hope for the manuscript he tossed in the backseat of his car. But at least, he said to himself, he'd given a grieving mother hope. He would read as much as he could endure, and then respond to her gently that it simply wasn't publishable.

That night, he gave the pages to his wife, Bunt. Hours later, she was still engrossed, and every so often he'd hear her laughing. She told her husband he must guide this novel to publication, that he simply mustn't let it die with its author. She loved how Toole just placed Ignatius into the scene, no introduction, no background, he's just there. And so, after reading it himself later that week and concurring, Walker Percy began his own crusade to unleash Ignatius upon the world.

For the next year and a half, Walker Percy persevered. Friends and colleagues saw little merit in a novel that no one could define. His own publisher, Farrar, Straus and Giroux, summarily dismissed it. Thelma, who was battling heart and kidney disease, was hospitalized and had to begin withdrawing her savings to pay medical bills. Then, in the spring of 1978, as the first test-tube baby was born, and John Travolta danced his way to back-to-back blockbusters, the tide finally shifted. A respected periodical in New Orleans, as a favor to Percy, published the first two chapters of the manuscript and the story of the ailing mother who wouldn't give up.

Soon after, a bookstore owner with dreams of becoming a publisher offered to bring the book to market. Then Louisiana State University suggested they might publish it. According to Louisiana's Napoleonic code, an archaic remnant of French rule, the law would compel J.D.'s relatives to try and thwart that publication, and a downtown editor in New York would change the game again.

LSU Press wasn't keen on taking chances. In 1979, university presses simply didn't publish fiction, but something about Ignatius Reilly captured the imagination of the company's acquisitions editor. Together with Walker Percy, who agreed to write a forward, they persuaded the reticent publisher at the small university press to make a leap of faith and, ideally, offload the paperback rights. The acquisitions editor then contacted Kent Carroll at Grove Press. Some months earlier, she'd sold him the paperback rights to a biography about a dictator's wife that most Americans had never heard of until *Evita* hit the bookshops. She was hoping she could sell him on Ignatius, too. Carroll wasn't as easily convinced this time around. Andrew Lloyd Webber wasn't getting ready to premiere a multi-million-dollar musical about Ignatius in London and New York. Still, he politely asked the editor about their plans to release Toole's novel, which he learned was set in New Orleans and featured a most unusual character. Carroll didn't find her answer convincing, but she pressed, and so a galley was soon on the way to his office.

The book arrived a few days later. The opening pages held more than Carroll anticipated: a singular character, more than unusual, at once both unique and immediately identifiable. It was dark outside when Carroll left the office, taking the galley with him. He stopped at the Lion's Head on his way home. As he enjoyed his dinner, then a cup of tea, he continued reading, fully engaged, captured by the novel's rare and irresistible humor until the bartender approached and asked that he not laugh so loud: customers were jealous. An hour later, and halfway through the manuscript, he returned home and read until midnight. He had trouble falling asleep. Daylight seemed too far away. The next morning, he went to Barney Rosset's office and explained why he wanted to acquire this *Confederacy of Dunces*. It was first and foremost, he explained to his boss, a rattling good story. Barney listened, as he had always before, then told his editor that he could do as he pleased as long as the advance payment didn't exceed two thousand dollars. Carroll made an offer to LSU that afternoon, increasing the amount slowly from one thousand to two thousand dollars as he added Canada and the United Kingdom onto the territories Grove would own.

The publisher at LSU Press was not optimistic about this strange book, admitting that if it weren't for Walker Percy agreeing to write the foreword, he would have passed on it. To a conservative university press, such an acquisition was a gamble, and so they allotted little time and resources to its launch. It was already the fall of 1979 and the hardcover was being released just a few months away in the spring. The book wasn't listed in the university press's catalog and only two outlets had ordered any, two hundred by Ingram, the national distributor based in Nashville, and twenty copies by the leading bookstore in New Orleans.

Carroll hoped that if he could leverage his relationships with the reviewers at the major newspapers and magazines and Grove's small but relentless sales force, he might be able to advance enough of the hardcovers to stores to ignite word of mouth. He knew he was taking a chance, that the book was problematic in parts and it adhered to virtually none of the literary conventions that were the standard upon which reviewers often formed their opinions. It was as if something or someone was urging him on, and he couldn't stop thinking about how he'd laughed when he'd read it.

The salespeople at LSU Press reluctantly sent him twenty, then fifty more bound galleys, which he delivered by hand to every influential book critic in New York and sent by first class mail to their counterparts in DC, Boston, Los Angeles, Chicago, and San Francisco, along with a personal letter. Within a few weeks, much to Carroll's relief, a flabbergasted university press had twenty-five hundred orders from independent stores, and two weeks later, five thousand orders from the big chain stores. Then the joyous reviews and articles in a dozen newspapers and magazines, such as *Time* and the *Washington Star*, arrived.

Two years had passed since Thelma's hospitalization. Her frail body belied the vibrant spirit within. Her son's masterpiece was being published. Some of J. D. Toole's relatives tried to prevent its publication, fearful that the book was about their family and might reflect poorly on them. Thelma owed a debt of thanks to the bookstore owner who'd intervened. How preposterous, Thelma thought, that they would assume Kenny would write about such a mundane, uneducated group of people. They demanded a manuscript, which Thelma refused to send. It was only when the bookstore owner mailed them her own copy and they saw for themselves that their concerns were without merit did they relinquish. The reason the bookstore owner had the manuscript was because she'd wanted to publish *A Confederacy of Dunces* herself after reading the article in the *New Orleans Review*, but she didn't have the means; and a pipedream, Thelma realized, wasn't going to put Kenny's book on the map. When LSU made an offer, the bookstore owner was disappointed. It wouldn't be the last she'd hear from J.D.'s ill-mannered brood, but Thelma wasn't thinking about that now. Soon, the moment for which she had been put on this earth would be here and she wanted to make her Kenny proud.

The year is 1981. The Iran Hostage Crisis has ended. President Ronald Reagan is shot. The first recognized cases of AIDS are identified, and Lady Diana Spencer marries Prince Charles of Wales. The month is April.

Kent Carroll was having dinner at The Front, a popular Village bar, watching the evening news on the overhead television set. When he heard the anchor informing viewers that the Pulitzer Prizes had been awarded that afternoon, and *A Confederacy of Dunces* was named the fiction winner, Carroll blurted out to the bartender, "Hey, my book just won the Pulitzer Prize!" The bartender toasted him with a free drink and announced to the other seated regulars that the guy down the bar just won the Pulitzer. Before the end of the evening, it was champagne all around and strangers being pulled in off the street to shake hands with the man who was somehow now a Nobel laureate.

Thelma was sitting in the lobby of the Omni Berkshire Hotel waiting to be escorted to *The Tomorrow Show* with Tom Snyder. Dressed in her Sunday best, she seemed almost giddy, like a child who'd just been told she got the lead in the school play. There was something about the way in which Thelma took to all the attention, the newspaper and radio interviews, the reviews, as if this moment belonged to her. Perhaps it was guilt, perhaps it was love, but whatever motivated Thelma Toole's performance, no one would have believed that she hadn't been the perfect mother.

The publicist from Grove Press greeted the limo as it pulled into NBC Studios. As she opened the passenger door, Thelma extended a white-gloved hand. An eager young production assistant was waiting for her at the stage door entrance. He was a year out of college, fresh and enthusiastic.

"I'd like to ask you a question, if that's okay."

Thelma nodded.

"I've read the book twice. It's living inside my head."

"It's a wonder and a mystery," she replied. "And, of course, it killed my son."

Subdued, he led her down a long hall to the green room. She would be talking about her beloved Kenny on live television with millions of people watching. This was her chance to share her boy's genius with the world. They'd never appreciated his intelligence, his artistic grace. But she would be the shining star illuminating his memory.

The green room was well stocked with food, and a caterer came in to replenish the bagels. Thelma was too nervous to eat. She could talk about her son as a child, but what if Mr. Snyder asked her about the defining moments in his life that spilled over onto the pages of his fiction? What if Mr. Snyder asked her about the days and weeks leading up to Kenny's suicide? She wouldn't talk about that, absolutely not. Yes, Thelma thought, this was like walking into a minefield.

The interview went well. Thelma held her own. She made the slight faux pas of looking into the camera instead of at Mr. Snyder for the first few questions, but when he politely corrected her, she continued on, delighting both him and his audience with her indefatigable love for her child. When she left the studio, a small crowd of people had gathered outside the door, pens in hand in anticipation of an autograph. If they couldn't obtain John Kennedy Toole's John Hancock, this was certainly the next best thing. Thelma smiled upon seeing the eager entourage and graciously signed each of their books: "With love, John Kennedy Toole."

The trip to New York to launch the paperback edition had been a whirlwind, and Thelma had soldiered through, paying little mind to her health. She had briefly considered following her doctors' advice and going on dialysis, but it would have interfered with the publicity junket that Grove had arranged.

She couldn't keep up with all the congratulatory cards and letters that had been flooding her mailbox since she'd returned home to New Orleans. Arthur would place them in a large basket next to the dining room table, where Thelma would sit and reply to each one. Arthur worried about his sister. She needed a cane to walk, and her pallor was as white as her talcum powder. He'd tried to hide the *New York Times* review of his nephew's book from Thelma, but she'd found it and read it, irritated with him for keeping it from her. Arthur didn't know what was worse: being the target of her wrath for trying to protect her or witnessing her sadness because he couldn't. The reviewer had accused both Kenny and Thelma of being anti-Semitic. Arthur found the notion ludicrous and encouraged Thelma to simply ignore it, as he was certain Kenny himself would have done. Thelma explained to her brother that she could endure any insult. "Perhaps I am an elitist but that doesn't make me an anti-Semite." Though they never spoke of the review again, Arthur noticed a flare of anger in Thelma's eyes whenever anyone mentioned the *New York Times*. It had been her Kenny's favorite newspaper.

With each passing week, Thelma watched her son's book climb the national best-seller lists, a bittersweet testimonial to what she'd known all along; that her child had been gifted. How ironic, she thought, that all her son's life she'd wanted greatness for him, and if she could have him back for just one more minute, to tell him how much she loved him, she wouldn't care about his achieving greatness anymore or winning a Pulitzer or being on best-seller lists, none of it would matter if she could only look upon his beautiful face, hear his voice once again. In May 1981, the Grove Press edition of *A Confederacy of Dunces* was No. 1 on the *New York Times* paperback best-seller list, which she couldn't understand, given their cruel review. Arthur had tried to explain that one had nothing to do with the other, that the book review was separate from the best-seller list, but it did little to diminish her frustration.

The year is 1983. The first mobile cellular phone call is made. Grenada is invaded by U.S. troops. *The Day After*, a made-for-television movie about the fallout of a nuclear disaster, airs on ABC, and meteorologists introduce audiences to the El Niño effect. There are now six hundred thousand Grove Press copies of *A Confederacy of Dunces* in circulation and the publisher has just ordered another print run of fifty thousand.

Thelma Toole was scribbling notes in her composition book, trying to assemble her thoughts for the letter she was preparing to write to her late husband's relatives. Thelma wanted *The Neon Bible* published. Her brother had finally given it to her after Kenny passed, telling her the story behind it, and she would be damned if those uneducated heathens would see a penny, especially not from something Kenny wrote when he was just a boy. "Where were these people when Kenny was growing up? Where were they when his father was sick and I was struggling to feed my family?" she thought. Thelma had already written the governor of Louisiana, a senator, and a handful of other politicians about the Napoleonic code, which allowed for such egregiousness to flourish. So she'd begun putting together a letter that she was hoping might shame J.D.'s family. Neither Thelma nor her husband's relatives could do anything with *The Neon Bible* unless both parties came to terms, as they each owned fifty percent of the rights. She realized she could trust no one with her grandchildren, which is how she saw Kenny's books. They were her son's progeny, and she would protect them from greed and ineptitude.

She'd handled everything. She'd willed her half of *The Neon Bible* to an old family friend in exchange for his promise to never allow anyone to publish it after her demise, and she'd given all of her son's school notebooks, personal correspondences, and the like to Tulane for their archives. She hesitated to give them the letters from Gottlieb, which she had come close to burning more than once, but decided, given the success of his book, that it was part of her son's legacy now. And she'd already made Arthur sign an agreement in which he relinquished all rights to her financial affairs. It's not that she didn't love her brother, but her first obligation was to Kenny.

Thelma had kept a secret from her brother. She had hidden it from everyone. She discovered it in the winter of 1973, a few days after she found *A Confederacy of Dunces*. She had gone back to Kenny's closet to finish cleaning it out when she came across another manuscript on the top shelf, way in the back, wedged between a box of baseball cards and a pile of old magazines. The story seemed to center around a hobo in Washington Square Park. Thelma read the first eighteen or twenty pages, then thumbed through the rest. There were at least three hundred additional pages. The final page abruptly stopped after two or three sentences and then behind it were another fifteen or twenty pages of notes. It was obviously incomplete but very close. She let it slide back down into the box and returned it to the shelf.

After *A Confederacy of Dunces* won the Pulitzer, she considered retrieving the unfinished manuscript and finishing it herself, but with her health in decline she was afraid she would die before she completed it and she couldn't entrust this sacred responsibility to anyone else. And so *Humphrey Wildblood*, the final book that Kenny would attempt to write, remained, in her closet, a mother and her son's little secret.

Greeley had been typing. The sun was just beginning to rise as he completed recording the last of his notes from his trip to New Orleans. He didn't enjoy living in Manhattan except on mornings like this, when a man could get a strong cup of coffee and a fresh bagel slathered with cream cheese before most diners in the rest of the country had turned their lights on. As he made his way down the three flights of stairs from his walk-up apartment in Chelsea, he hummed to himself despite not having slept all night. His article for the *Daily News* on John Kennedy Toole was coming alive. He'd found enough to support his theory. When he got back to his typewriter, he was ticking off the elements of the story in his head.

Kent Carroll had given him some interesting stuff. When Greeley called about an interview, the editor didn't hesitate to help. One of Greeley's biggest challenges had been finding folks who could remember details from twenty-five years ago. Carroll's recollection of events was vivid, and he seemed to enjoy talking about his connection to the book. They met at the White Horse Tavern on Hudson Street, which both men found especially fitting. Kent talked about the book's launch, the success of the hardcover, and the surprising reaction from the university press.

"The publisher at Southern Louisiana University was angry?" Greeley asked.

"Yes, furious."

"Didn't they sell something like forty thousand copies of the book?"

"They did indeed and for a first novel, it's even more extraordinary, but that's not what the publisher found upsetting. Some of the book reviewers mistakenly said the hardcover was published by Grove Press because they had dealt with me. The publisher called Barney Rosset complaining. And Barney wasn't thrilled, either. There's a lot of ego at work. He didn't like the fact that people in the business were talking about the novel that his editor had discovered. I didn't discover it. Walker Percy did. I just believed in its potential and needed to protect Grove's investment in the paperback."

"What happened after all that?"

Carroll smiled. "Barney called me into his office and said that he didn't think we could work together anymore. So I packed my things, and a colleague of mine and I started our own publishing house."

"Do you harbor any bitterness?" Greeley asked. "I mean, if I would have discovered a book that made everyone tons of money and gotten fired for it, I would have been furious."

"I wasn't happy, but I wasn't as resentful as I might have been. I got a lot out of my years at Grove and I was grateful for that. It was time for me to start anew. It's interesting how things work out."

Greeley and Carroll left the White Horse that night still talking about publishing. Greeley was intrigued that Carroll described the industry not as a business at all, but more of an exciting handicraft.

"A lot of it is just good fortune and intuition," Kent explained.

"Do you think *A Confederacy of Dunces* would have had the same success if it had been published in 1965?"

"I don't think so, no. The world wasn't ready for Ignatius Reilly then any more than it would have been ready for Bluto Blutarsky if *Animal House* had been released in the sixties. It was a different generation. It begs the question, even though it was a far inferior book, if *Superworm* had been published in the eighties, would it have done better?"

"You're only the second person I've met who's ever even heard of that novel. The first was my mentor, a professor at NYU."

"Have you read it?"

"Yeah, and it was nearly impossible to get a copy as it's been out of print so long. I had to order a used library copy from Amazon. Funny that Robert Gottlieb published that book and not *Dunces*."

Greeley also spoke with the man who fought for *A Confederacy of Dunces* to receive the Pulitzer Prize in 1981. One of the most respected literary figures in the country, having reviewed for the *Washington Post* for almost a quarter century, Jonathan Yardley served as chairman of the nominating committee for fiction that year. The prestigious award had never been given to an author posthumously and Greeley wanted to hear what happened behind closed doors all those years ago. He had imagined a dramatic scene like something out of the movie *12 Angry Men*, with shaking fists and impassioned speeches and a lone champion taking on the establishment risking everything to fight for what's right.

He was surprised to learn that the members of the committee were unanimous in their recommendation that Toole receive the award. While there were a lot of exceptional books that year, including William Maxwell's *So Long, See You Tomorrow*; Frederick Buechner's *Godric*; and Anne Tyler's *Morgan's Passing*, the committee agreed that it was the most deserving on its literary merits alone. They also felt the repeated rejection the novel had endured was an injustice and that if it won, it would send a message. The only tricky part was how to position it to the Pulitzer Board. *A Confederacy of Dunces* was unconventional in every way and the jurors didn't want what happened with Duke Ellington, back in the sixties, to happen again. Ellington was nominated but the board rejected the nomination. At the time, jazz wasn't considered weighty enough for a Pulitzer. It wasn't until Wynton Marsalis was awarded the prize three decades later that a jazz composition won. Ellington was honored with a special citation posthumously. Greeley wondered if Kenny paved the way for Ellington.

———

It is 1984. *Terms of Endearment* sweeps the Academy Awards. The Soviet Union boycotts the Summer Olympics. Bruce Springsteen releases his seventh album, *Born in the U.S.A.* The "minivan" debuts in America. The month is August.

The funeral made national news. Thelma Ducoing Toole, mother of John Kennedy Toole, was dead. The service, befitting someone important, was open to the public. Some came to pay their respects; others to fulfill their curiosity about a woman they'd never met but whom they had read about somewhere. Arthur sat quietly in the back of the room, wondering when it would be considered socially acceptable for him to go home. He'd had enough of all the reporters and photographers, the gawkers, as he liked to call them, asking him questions he didn't want to answer, and offering condolences that he didn't feel comfortable accepting from strangers. The last few weeks had been exhausting, back and forth to the hospital, waiting, always waiting for when he would have to wait no more. He'd felt guilty upon hearing of her passing. His sister had relegated him to the sidelines of her life, yet still expected him to meet her every demand. His reaction had been relief. He'd done some reading and learned this was not an uncommon response to the loss of a family member, particularly one like Thelma, who had been sick and dependent a long time.

He'd gone to the storage unit intending to go through her things, maybe donate some items to her church, but when he saw all those boxes piled on top of one another, the familiar handwriting describing the contents of each, he felt as she must have felt when her Kenny died. He'd loved Kenny, but Thelma was Arthur's person in the way that Kenny had been hers, and when you lose that one person who's your everything, despite whatever may have happened between you, a part of you dies along with them. Standing there in that storage unit, alone with nothing but the remnants of a life now wrapped in tissue paper and taped shut, Arthur Toole grieved.

At the advice of a friend, he called Catholic Charities, gave them a key to the unit, and told them to take whatever they could use, that it's what his sister would have wanted, and asked if they would kindly unburden him of the rest. A few weeks later, he received a package. It contained a thank-you note and a faded manuscript with scribbles all over it and the name *Humphrey Wildblood* scrawled across the bottom that they thought he might want to have.

That night, Arthur did something had hadn't done in a very long time. He poured himself a sherry from Thelma's favorite bottle, a rare vintage from Spain that he'd given her for her birthday. He lifted his glass high and toasted his sister and brother-in-law and his nephew, who were finally at peace. Then he retired to his room and began to read. In the street below, passersby could hear someone laughing through an open window.

⸻

Greeley was going over his piece for the *Daily News* one last time before he filed. It was spring of 2004 and almost a lifetime since Kenny had written *A Confederacy of Dunces*. Greeley checked all his facts. He was satisfied with his work. He knew now there was a book in all of this. He envisioned doing it as a memoir, perhaps a novel. He was confident in a way he'd never been. Kenny and Ignatius had silenced his father. Greeley was free. He had never felt so ready for anything. He was heading back to New Orleans in a few weeks. His contact at Tulane had emailed, telling him that there was talk of a lost work of Toole's, and he was hoping if he did come across anything in his research that he would let them know. Greeley had heard rumors before but not given them much credence. That Tulane University thought it might be possible changed things. Of this he was certain: if a long-lost manuscript by Toole did exist, he would find it.

⸻

The article made the front page of the Sunday entertainment section. The managing editor of the *Daily News*, after reading the first draft, had requested another two thousand words and a photo spread. Within hours of publication, the story was all over the internet. There were offers for television and radio interviews, an opportunity to coproduce a documentary, requests for speaking engagements.

Professor Bell called to congratulate his protégé, inviting him for celebratory drinks at the Knickerbocker. Two bottles of wine later and a sumptuous dinner followed by a rare cognac, the two friends parted for the evening. Greeley decided to walk back to his apartment. As he made his way to Chelsea, his mind kept returning to a piece of the puzzle that remained a mystery. Kenny's last stop on that final sojourn. All roads pointed to Flannery O'Connor's home in Georgia. Greeley had gone there hoping to find someone who might remember Kenny, but it was too long ago and most of the people who had worked there at the time had long since died or moved on. Greeley spent the day touring the plantation, taking it all in, trying to imagine what Kenny felt as he strolled the beautifully manicured, sprawling grounds; and if it was there, where his favorite writer walked and breathed and lived and died, if he'd sought her blessing for the sacrifice he knew that he must make.

March 1969

Kenny had the road map open in the passenger seat. He'd take his time, enjoy the rest of the drive. His visit with Flannery had been more than he'd expected. He'd felt her presence sure as he felt the first stirrings of spring and its promise of renewal. As the tranquil fields of Andalusia faded into his rear-view mirror, happy images flashed across his memory like bits of film, one blending into the next: catching his first fastball with his dad; his mama's arms around him holding him tight after he'd had a bad dream; sharing secrets with Uncle Arthur, who never told; long, slow kisses with Ellen; drinking with Joel until dawn, laughing until their sides hurt; catfishing on the bayou with Gator; his fingers dancing across the keys of a typewriter and the sound of Ignatius coming to life.

ACKNOWLEDGMENTS

The authors would like to thank the following people:

The gracious staff at the Tulane University Archives.

Cory McLaughlin, the author of *Butterfly in the Typewriter*, for his valuable research.

Joel Fletcher, for his insights about Kenny Toole and his Southern hospitality.

Our publisher Claiborne Hancock, his colleagues Jessica Case and Lauren Rosenthal, and the team at Pegasus Books.

Michael Szromba, for his unwavering encouragement.

Raonaid Ryn, for her keen literary instincts.

And lastly and most importantly, Helen Whitney, for most everything. She made this a better book.

BOOK CLUB
READING GROUP GUIDE

QUESTIONS FOR DISCUSSION

1. *A Confederacy of Dunces* was published in 1980, sixteen years after it was written. Do you think if it was published in 1964 it would have achieved the same success?

2. Why do you think the authors included the character of Ignatius?

3. The authors suggest that Kenny sacrificed his life so that his work could live on. Do you think that other writers and artists who died by suicide and achieved recognition post-humously might have experienced a similar motivation?

4. Do you believe there's a lost manuscript somewhere?

5. Do you agree with the authors' choice to write a novel instead of a biography?

6. What did Ignatius see in Kenny that he couldn't see in himself?